# THE LETTER FROM PENOBSCOT MILLS

### A NOVEL BY
## PHILIP BOUCHARD

America Star Books
*Frederick, Maryland*

Softcover 9781635082319
PUBLISHED BY AMERICA STAR BOOKS, LLLP
www.americastarbooks.pub
Frederick, Maryland

# DEDICATION

This novel is dedicated to my wife,
Sandra who likes how I write.

## AUTHOR'S NOTE

I have written *A Letter from Penobscot Mills* in eight short stories that do not appear in chronological order although the first story begins the saga. The ninth and final chapter ties the story together. The novel spans about twenty four years in the lives of individuals in a small paper mill town in northern Maine. Five boys of a similar age play their parts. This tale is not of the small town but of certain individuals for what I enjoy most is manufacturing characters. Each person has a perspective unlike the others and sees from a unique emotional frame. Much of the novel is dedicated to building a collective witness to events in their lives.

Philip Bouchard
Philip.bouchard@yahoo.com

# TABLE OF CONTENTS

# A MURDER OF CROWS

Puffs of yellow dust escaped from between her toes and her bare feet extended a dance that her firm tanned legs had started, as she walked down the dirt road toward our house. A short print dress accompanied her dance the way a three piece combo sways to its own inner music at the roadhouse only a half mile away. The early morning sun lit the stage, reflecting off her strewn hair and shoes dangling down her back. Her legs posed too far apart for propriety's sake, the sun, the dress, and the oddest of smiles cast a shadow on more than the dusty road that July morn.

This would be the summer that would teach me guilt, a guilt which now draws me to write a record of this small portion of life. I did not then comprehend fully the events of that summer. It has taken me years to wash an undeserved sin from my heart and provide a cooler detached perspective. Truly I was not to blame and I could not have done anything to prevent those events, yet I felt the keenest stab of guilt I would ever know. Guilt – that emperor of an emotion, inserts himself effortlessly within you, without regard to truth or fairness, to reside with you, not doing any damage himself, but simply living in your bedroom, making you do all the work of shame. And so I hope that by portraying Cassius, I may now calculate the ordinate and the abscissa of those events through stretched eye slits, carefully watching without emotion for the moment I might stab Caesar.

The events of that July were, to me, like the first time I saw my father fell a large white pine by the river behind our house. The sixty or so feet stood straight, firm, proud against an azure sky. I had scrambled up her often, hid from the sun's heat, and swung from her branches to finally rest 'neath her canopy on cool spongy earth. From the first cracking yelp, through the groan that seemed to take a life-time (and most surely took a life), to the final thrash of branches and thud against the ground, I consciously knew, "This was death."

Angela McLean, as it was often said of her, was a fine figure of a woman, though she was only fourteen years old. Why anyone would consider it proper to call a fourteen year old girl a "figure of a woman" I could not guess but I had heard it often. I was ten at the time. As I watched her walk the path to our house early that morning, she pointed her toes at each step and lolled her head back in a private reverie. She had enjoyed the night of dancing, barefoot mostly, on a dusty wooden floor; enjoyed the loud music that shut out another world, and fairly marveled at the attention she was paid by men of dubious virtue. But she never saw the lack of virtue in those men or anyone; probably not even when it was too late. She was a girl in whom there was not guile.

She was my sister who laughed with me and played paper dolls, made baby talk when she felt shy or embarrassed, and squinted real hard when asked a question by her teacher. She provided an appropriate and intense sign of concentration but alas, she rarely had any idea as to the answer. So long ago had she failed to comprehend, that she did not bother to search for any answer. For if she tripped over it in her limited grasp of knowledge, she wouldn't recognize it anyway. Angela was slow, some said simple, retarded, teched in the head, and beautiful. For her trouble she garnered slurs, disdain and lust. But she was also harmless, generous, friendly, caring. I loved my sister.

Our father would have beaten her if he had known she had been at the roadhouse again. He would have beaten me for knowing and not telling. I now understand that it was the beatings when she was little that had blunted her ability. I'm sure she would have turned into something quite wonderful too. Her intelligence may have been blunted, but her soul was truly artistic. She could draw and paint, but most of all she could dance. Her whole body expressed everything she felt. This was not a skill that was prized in our town, but if she had any chance to attend a conservatory she would have been spectacular. But that was "bull shit" according to my father. Father worked in the paper mill piling laps (pulp logs) to feed the life of our small paper mill town, Penobscot Mills, and was on the grave yard shift not yet due home. Mom had been long since gone from our lives. I never knew where.

About a month before Angela danced at the roadhouse she and I were walking to the town hall. The flap of loose leather from the bottom of my shoe scraped loudly against the tarred road and concrete steps. "Hey, Pauli-baby, Pauli-baby," taunted a much older boy one could only call a bully. "Where ya goin', Pauli-baby, cry-baby?" Angela and I had often endured the stench of Johnny Watson.

The resident tough, Johnny Watson was as belligerent and emotionally conflicted as Billy Bigalow but meaner. At ten I didn't cry anymore but I had often, under the jab of his knuckles in my back as he held me down and rammed the knuckle of his middle finger into my spine. Held by the hair I yelped. Running away I wept. Walking quickly past his house, he barked the frustrated howl of a cur tied to a post, unable to hunt, run, devour. I ignored Johnny as if he were a dog tied safely in his front yard because he was mowing the lawn. I knew this was a chore set upon him by his father and a task which he dared not abandon, for Johnny feared only his father, yet ever his father. We were headed for the town hall, anyway.

Many people had gathered to listen to the police chief, Harold Pister, talk about what they were going to do about Old Blisters who lived out at the town dump. Old Blisters sort of took care of the Penobscot Mills dump you might say. At least he lived in a shack he'd fashioned of the dump itself; build right into the side of a huge mound of stink. The discarded scabs of our small town were piled and chinked into an enormous slag heap of rotted refuse. Tunneled out and laid over with corrugated tin, Blisters had carved a home. Needless to say as long as Old Blisters stayed at the dump no one was bothered by him. But this summer he had taken to the habit of visiting Main Street and sitting outside the drug store.

"He just sits on the curb and don't talk to no one," Mr. Watson was saying, "but he stinks to high heaven and I'd swear he carries them rats with him in that sack. I think I seen the sack move."

Angela moved closer to Mr. Watson. Sometimes it seemed she could understand people better if she was real close to them when they were speaking. But she got too close to Mr. Watson. When he saw her he said, "Blisters ain't got no right for living', no more than this teched girl do."

"Yep, yep," the crowd agreed and Mr. Watson shoved Angela down the cement steps of the town hall. Mine were the only eyes that cared but I dared not do anything to help.

Angela crept off slowly and I joined her around the corner where the grass was sweet and shade had begun to lean against the building. I sat down next to her noticing her knee was bleeding a little. She was picking at it with studied interest. The smell of the grass was sweet, I remember, and the kindest of breezes made Angela's bangs jump. Even at ten, I felt bad not having done anything to help her. But I said to myself, 'She's got to learn not to stick her face in so close.'

A raucous and riotous blast came from around the corner and I jumped. I guess I was still scared. Looking up from Angela's wound I glimpsed Johnny Watson. He saw us as he came from mowing the lawn and spat. He swaggered purposefully using his very presence to intimidate his friends walking with him, Buster Moze and Ralphie Pister, the chief's son. I jumped up and took off. Angela followed. We ran hard but Angela looked back once. Six eyes tracked our escape as dispassionately as gray wolves track their prey; this time choosing to simply mark the path and move on to the crowd at the town hall. They weren't hungry yet.

I heard later that day, that the crowd agreed to "do something" about Old Blisters but nobody felt strong enough to go near him. Looking back I believe that was the beginning, the real beginning. When the appetites of stupid, angry men are frustrated, the anger sits at the bottom of their stomachs and on top of their reason.

Bartlett's Drug store sat on the corner of Main and leaned up the hill toward Beech Street. It contained everything I needed: ice cream, soda pop, and candy. My only income came from scouring the town for soda pop bottles discarded by someone unable to grasp the importance of the two cents I could redeem them for. Once in a great while I'd find a five cent bottle, one of the big ones I had never owned in my life. I thought it inconceivable that anyone could drink so large amount, let alone toss the bottle in the grass unredeemed.

Approaching Bartlett's with Angela I spied the neck of a five cent bottle poking over the rim of the curb. I reached for it and found it connected to something – Old Blisters. Resting up against the trashcan in front of Bartlett's, Old Blisters was holding the bottle by the base. He made a clucking sound in his throat as if to say, "No, no, it's mine." I froze. Held by his gaze, I was no less a prisoner than that of the "Ancient Mariner," who was held by the words, "There was a ship," and held by the shaft of a five cent pop bottle as well. We stared at one another with reciprocal fascination. Staring down those eyes the color of pale green milk glass, weeping a bit at the corners, I thought I saw, not a ram shackled creature self-fashioned of corrugated tin and filth, but a forgotten man. I could just see the ragged remnants of a dream – an ambition or two. Then he smiled. To be sure it was a toothless smile.

He let go of the bottle and with an endearing gesture, offered it to me. He pulled his burlap sack toward him and I too saw movement. Carefully glancing at Angela I noticed her total and rapt attention as Old Blister reached into the bag. A suffocating disgust poured into my stomach when he pulled out, not a live rat as I has expected, but another five cent bottle. His bag was filled with them – each one wrapped in brown paper.

"That's a nickel's worth," he said. "And I got 28 of 'em here in my pouch. You kin have that if you take these inside and git my money," jabbing his thumb toward Bartlett's. "Don't quite know how much it is but it's more than I got now. Do you know how much it is?" He asked shyly.

"A dime short of a dollar fifty," I said. "One dollar and forty cents."

Old Blisters leaned back against the trash can, closed his eyes and smiled. "Can't git it myself 'cause they won't let me in." It was strange to me that I immediately liked Old Blisters and wanted to help him. But before I could move, Angela picked up the sack and started dragging it toward the door. The muffled sound of the paper covered bottles rolling around in the sack didn't sound like glass but like a low animal sound from the throat of something sick and dying. I shuddered remembering what we had thought might be in the sack.

Angel pulled at the heavy door. Dragging the sack over the threshold, she backed into Bartlett's and backed into Mr. Watson. He had entered the drug store for a pack of smokes and stood grinning; soiled tee shirt and work pants, sweat stained from a shift on the pulp pile. He reached into his mouth and picked off a bit of tobacco from his tongue and reached down and picked up Angela by the waist, holding her breast as he did.

"Well look here what I found," said Mr. Watson, as he began to nuzzle her neck.

He had Angela just off the floor and reached down to her belly, pulling at her dress all the while. Angela kicked and began thrashing as Mr. Watson pulled her dress up over her head and Angel hung there in her panties, not being able to see, as he and Mr. Bartlett laughed.

Angela pushed her dress down below her waist and stood and stared at Mr. Watson. They looked at each other for some time as if they had just recognized each other from somewhere and couldn't remember where. Then Mr. Watson spun Angela around, goosed her up the behind with his finger and shoved her out the door.

"Oh, sweet pussy, that is," he grinned and sniffed his finger. But his grin faded as Angela, bouncing toward the street, ran into Old Blisters. Blisters held her in the fatherly fashion I had never seen my father do and glared at Mr. Watson. If I had ever seen *High Noon* with Gary Cooper, this was surely a skewed version of it. One sweat stained hulk staring down another ragged and soiled figure.

No one said anything until I tried to step around Mr. Watson to retrieve the sack of 5 cent bottles. "What're you doin' son?" said Mr. Watson peering down at me.

"Just gittin' the sack," I said and I moved deliberately and steadily hoping for no confrontation. I grabbed the sack and started toward the counter where Mr. Bartlett stood chewing on a small cigar stub.

"Git them rats outta here," he shouted to nobody in particular.

"Ain't my job to touch 'em," said Mr. Watson.

"They're not rats," I said, "they're bottles," and I pulled one out of the sack. But wrapped in dirty brown paper that had been scuffed from the dragging, it could have looked like something dead and stiff.

"Git them out," shouted Mr. Bartlett.

"Alright, Bill, I'll git 'em," bellowed Mr. Watson and he heaved both me and the sack onto the sidewalk. I heard both me and the bottles crack.

By now others had gathered and were shouting, mostly at us. Johnny Watson came around the corner, eyed Angela, then his father, then Angela, then his father once again. Seeing Johnny, Mr. Watson just swung around to face us.

"Git, you filthy slut girl, git!" Mr. Watson hollered again and we ran --two kids and part of a man, scrambling down the street, heading toward the dump.

Through the field and around the woods, we were out of sight. It was quite a group that trooped to Old Blisters. Neither Angela nor I said anything and what Old Blisters was saying didn't make any sense. He just sort of kept singing to himself. It might have been a foreign language for all I knew or one he'd made up in the desperate search for himself.

Once inside Old Blisters' house, it didn't seem so grotesque. The floor was scrap linoleum. He had a table and chairs to eat on, a stove for cooking and heating, and a couch. To my surprise he had a busted end table that was spliced together with a stray piece of white pine log and I recognized it as our end table that got busted when my dad came home drunk, tripped and landed right on it. He had me haul it to the dump on my bike. Now it was resurrected in Old Blisters' house.

Blisters kept singing while I told Angela she should stay away from Mr. Watson. She said, "OK, OK, OK!" over and over again.

Over the next couple of weeks we began to visit Old Blisters frequently. No one chose to follow us, so we didn't bother hiding what we did. But wolves marked our path and progress to be sure. Angela and Old Blisters seemed to chat for hours on end, about nothing I guessed. I still understood only some of what Old Blisters said but Angela got on well with him – like they were speaking the same sing-song language. They connected on a level that came from beneath the earth, deep in an echoing cavern, two halves of one scrambled up brain. Truth was Old Blisters became more of a father than we ever had. Even when we weren't at Blisters' place, we spied him peeking around corners at us. Sometimes up in a tree, he was like the owl that lived atop of his shack, just staring. Old Blister told us that he mended that owl's wing when it was little but he couldn't fly real well. But it wasn't much of a trip from the roof to a nearby rat at the dump.

Days drifted and swayed atop white pines or on our backs in a field behind the high school and chinked themselves into freedom and peace with sandwiches under a lemon sun. Days that only summer can give with Angela and Old Blisters fishing Spencer's creek for brook trout or searching for arrow heads and pop bottles. I liked summer days. But the nights...

The wooden screen door creaked at 4:30 in the morning and I awoke with a start. Our father couldn't be home yet. No, it was Angela again. Gripping the linoleum with bare toes, she crept into her bed next to mine. I knew where she had been and I lay there breathing slowly when the shadow came and began kissing her. The shadow had apparently visited before since it knew just where to go in the darkened room. The shadow began reaching under Angela's dress, but she wasn't fighting like that day in the drug store with Mr. Watson. The shadow was there for a minute, no more, when Old Blisters grabbed it, slid it across the linoleum and out the door. The shadow ran. It was over. It was quiet. I didn't move. Old Blisters was gone, the shadow was gone, Angela just lay there.

I had seen my sister naked before. Anyone living in a real small house suffers a lack of privacy. I knew about the secret hair between her legs and had my own sinful thoughts any boy would. Fascination and fear are exciting together. Throw in curiosity and you've got a young boy's chemistry alright. But I still didn't move, not until our father came home.

I decided to take a walk down town and hang around by myself for a while. A few men coming off the graveyard shift like our father were talking by the town hall. They were saying something about shutting down a shift and what would they do. Then Mr. Watson came by and began talking about the road house and Angela.

"You shoulda seen that girl dance. Like she was crazy. But she ain't crazy I tell ya. She knows what she's doing. And I think she's been doing it with my boy."

"Haw, haw, haw" cawed the group of sweaty, soiled men.

There was no place in my brain to put this information. All I knew at the time was Angela had been "messing around" with Johnny Watson. I didn't really understand then what that meant but that made it all the more disturbing. The sun was well up and I sat in the grass across from the drug store. I loved my sister and do to this day. I didn't sort out what I was thinking then but looking back I realize I was angry for the way people and Johnny Watson were taking advantage of Angela. But she had to learn.

Angela showed up then and was exactly the same as any other day. Probably nothing had happened as far as she was concerned. We walked out to the dump to get something to eat. A vague undefined feeling kept sweeping through my brain. I was both disturbed and titillated at the thoughts I was having. Angela began to sing and dance. When she twirled, her dress came up and I saw she didn't have underpants on. But she usually didn't. I stopped, held her arms, and looked in her eyes.

"You've got to stop going to the road house. Do you understand? Those guys are not your friends. You're gonna git into trouble."

"OK, OK, OK." Angela just kept saying.

I smiled, hugged her and we walked on to Old Blisters.

The next week was disturbing. Once walking in back of the drug store I saw a dead cat hanging by its tail, beaten and one eye dangling out of its socket. I didn't look but a glimpse, but that picture has stuck with me to this day. Another time our father yanked me out of bed and said, "Git up. Git dressed quick we're gonna go shooting"

"Now?" I asked. It was maybe five in the morning of one of our father's days off.

"Git those shoes on and git out the door, you ain't gonna miss this."

I dashed out the door and there were a whole group of men with guns. My father shoved my 410 in my hand and a couple of shells and loaded his double barrel. Then the group, more like a mob, walked off quickly toward the old abandoned sand pit. The sand pit was abandoned early because there wasn't much sand so it was a real narrow gorge with high banks. Mr. Pickard, a farmer, had cornered several families of foxes and sent his son to get help. Mr. Pickard, Mr. Watson, Chief Pister, my father, several other boys and men and me stared into that dark gorge. Then Chief Pister turned on his light on the cop car catching glowing eyes darting this way and that.

Everyone opened fire at once. My father slapped me on the head and I fired. I don't know how long this went on but I know not one of those foxes came out.

When we got back I told Angela about it. I remember I cried a little and she held me. Angela, Old Blisters and I went the next day to look. You just have to look don't you? I don't know how many foxes there were. It was like there was only one fox in a heap. Days later people were still talking and telling jokes about that night. They said it was justified – not a crime at all. I got sick.

The third thing was a clincher. Apparently, as I've pieced together the story after so many years, our father found out about Angela dancing and "everything" at the road house. Four or five in the morning he burst into the house, grabbed Angela by the hair and began punching her in the chest. She thrashed and swung until he let her go. Then he grabbed me.

"D'you know about this?" he screamed. My first broken nose but worse was a bruised groin. My nuts hurt so badly. Then, drunken, he passed out.

For a while after that we went back to sandwiches under a lemon sun. We went back to lying on our backs in the field and playing hide and seek in the woods. I began to like summer days again.

But as I said, she pointed her toes at each step and lolled her head back in a private reverie. Angela's shape was easy to see that morning, just before sun up, but other shapes I've had to guess at all these years, for out of the woods came a shadow I took to be Johnny Watson but thicker somehow. He began pulling at her dress and pawing her. She was thrashing back and her dress got half torn off.

You have to know I was only ten and all of this took only one maybe two minutes. And then Old Blisters literally dropped out of a nearby tree and swung at the shadow. Now the shadow was joined by three slimmer figures. A tussle, a stray white pine log, a thrashing of limbs, and Angela and Old Blisters lay on the dusty road alone.

My father said they killed each other because they were lovers. So did Chief Pister and everyone else. "Good to have them both gone." As incredulous and is seems, everyone accepted as fact that two people could bludgeon each other to death thus demonstrating how little regard they had for the retarded girl and the hobo.

When I started to open my mouth to talk about the other shadows who surely were Ralphie, Buster, Johnny and Mr. Watson, (though I couldn't be sure) my father held me by the throat against the wall and his words sprayed whisky in my face, "You say one word to disgrace this family..."

After that I said nothing. It is the sin I've come to confess. Nothing for maybe a month. No words. Nothing for my sister. Nothing for Old Blisters. Nothing.

I was ten but I'm not anymore.

Angela is buried by the river behind the house, though the house isn't there anymore. I visit every day and sit and watch the water dance over rocks and limbs and smiles of sunlight.

I come home from the graveyard shift in the morning to some rooms above a store. I cross the linoleum to the window. The early morning sun casts shadows that chill me. And I drink -- and pet a cat I've named Angela.

# MAIDEN AUNT

Pictures, black and whites
Mute faces long born
Cast shadows on carpet,
Old but not worn.

Pictures, black and whites
Hung straight to the floor
Maiden Aunt on her night watch
Did she ever want more?

Piano keys well dusted
Yet never thus played
Songs of the heart
Forever dismayed

But out in her garden
Flowers sway in the breeze
He wished he could have one,
Must only say please.

Great marches they took
Past the house, past the corner
Off to the graveyard
To practice a mourner.

As a child he stared
At the pictures those nights
Maiden Aunt on the night watch
Of pictures, black and whites

The shadow of white pine trees, the caress of the breeze, and
the quiet, stilled breath of expectancy walked with his Aunt as

he watched her reach the corner. A black sedan slowed and stopped. She opened the door, turned, smiled, threw a quick vigorous wave and was gone.

When he was twelve David White went to live with his Aunt Dot in Brunswick, Maine.

His mother stopped the car in front, leaned across him and opened the door. "You know I can't keep you. Dot's nice. Here's your suit case." She handed him a small child size case with not very much in it. He barely got out of the car when she drove off. David White approached the door and knocked. "Are you David?" his Aunt asked. He nodded. "Then come in."

Dorothy Tebbits lived in a house that was a one and a half story Cape Cod with dormers and grey wooden siding and yellow trim. The backyard was large with oak, a white picket fence and a garden. Bowdoin College, the swinging bridge, tall straight white pines, and the cemetery became David's playground. He slept on the sofa in the living room, his Aunt Dot upstairs in her room, though he was not sure if she ever slept. Deep quiet nights, old carpet, and the tick of a clock on the mantel made for a peaceful sleep, but there was ever the creak and footfall of Aunt Dot. She crept through the house rearranging bric-a-brac, dusting unseen crannies and staring at the black and white pictures on the wall over the piano which was never played.

Photography in 1957 was not what it is today. All of the pictures were black and white, color being a wasteful expense. A *Brownie* camera served just fine and the memories of those images would only require a gentle tap to spill into the eyes and heart. He watched his Aunt with fascination do that many times those nights, tapping one photo then another. He didn't know who many of those people were; great aunts and uncles, old friends all captured in stilted emotionless black frames, daring you to smile. There was one of a man and woman standing in front of a telegraph pole impatient for the click of the shutter. Another of an old woman sitting in a fabric upholstered rocking chair. Her face clearly said, "What are you doing in my house."

David began to know a few of the pictures though: Mr. Getchal, Mr. Newell, and Professor Douglas. He called them his Aunt's boyfriends. He didn't really think they were her boyfriends at first, but they visited them often, never at the house. No one lived with Dot and David or visited. His Grandmother and Grandfather died in 1953 and his Aunt Dot, the fifth child of seven, stayed to be their caretaker and execute a vigil which witnessed them slip into quiet death on the same day in their very own bed. Dot never married and martyred her life to their care. For that she earned the house, a yellow 1941 Ford Super Deluxe Coupe, and a small inheritance which she frugally administered.

They took walks most days, weather permitting. Summer they would walk in the morning. During school months she would pick David up in the Coupe, drive home and begin their walk. "Walks-a-talks" she called them. She did most of the talking and he learned a lot. He learned how to properly steam clams and lobster, fish chowder always began with frying salt pork, you should have 13 points to open a bridge hand (always), and a New England Boiled Dinner required rutabaga. His Aunt Dot also taught David White how to feel, how to love, and how to hurt.

David heard his new shoes snap against the tar sidewalk and his Aunt's shoes squish. She wouldn't let him wear sneakers or loafers, "They are not good for your feet." Her shoes were New England "Walkers." David's shoes were all leather, uppers and soles. She got him a pair of black and one of brown soon after his mother abandoned him. At the corner was a favorite grove of pine standing in a vacant lot, whispering to each other the secrets of Indians who once lived there. Straight on across Main Street to Bowdoin College, the pair sauntered lightly on Longfellow's earth.

Who was this lady with whom he would eventually spend eleven years, David wondered? She required shoes to be worn in the house, bed time was strictly enforced, the table must be set before each meal (including breakfast) with a knife (sharp blade pointing in toward the plate), fork, spoon and napkin. You couldn't go outside in the summer mornings until the dew had dried and they played cards or read each night. Coming from Penobscot Mills, a small paper mill town in the woods of Maine, David was the waif of the town. He had little structure with his mother. She was unmarried. David White never knew his father – a soldier on leave, his mother would only say – presumably somebody named White. Rules were new to David after being raised so loosely but not unwelcome.

So there he was on his third walk with his Aunt Dot drifting past the Bowdoin Library's concrete steps heading toward one of several stone buildings. The pair stayed on the walk, never on the grass. Aunt Dot's rules were more of a comfort to him eventually. Even though his mother provided the slimmest of upbringings he still felt abandoned, and Dot's rules wrapped around him – manifesting care if not love. Rather than entering through the front of the building, she led David to the left and down a half flight of stone steps, through a wooden door to a hallway. His Aunt Dot peeked through the window of the first door on the left, smiled and entered, asking him to wait. Pipes were exposed at the ceiling and he heard the building breathing. The chemical odor was formaldehyde and it seeped into David's stomach.

The door creaked open and Aunt Dot beckoned. He crossed the threshold and glimpsed something naked and dead floating in a huge jar which made him stop and cringe. "That's just a baby pig, nothing to worry about," said his Aunt in a manner he would come to find comforting many times later.

"Professor, this is David my nephew. David, this is Professor Winston Douglas. He's a professor of biology here at Bowdoin."

"Hello," David mumbled.
"Good to meet you. How long will you be staying?" asked Professor Douglas.
Looking at his Aunt he admitted, "I don't know."
"Well, Brunswick's a nice place to visit or live. Look around the lab,"
said Douglas.

His Aunt Dot and Professor Douglas continued talking about events at the college as David explored the walls of this moldy and disturbing room. Stuffed animals of most any kind were displayed alongside great jars of drowned and suffocated creatures, floating without dignity, unable to avoid shame. They drank their formaldehyde and stared at him. They were not horrified at being thus entombed – rather resigned to a fate of watching. He saw the eye of a small beaver wink, sending terror through his belly.

"David, dear, we need to go, so if you would please wait outside for a minute, I'll be with you shortly," said Aunt Dot.

He gratefully left, mumbling a 'nice to meet you' and found himself in the hall. After a few minutes his Aunt joined him. Out the door and up the stone steps to sunlight, they were emerging from a tomb. The pair squished and snapped through the campus and ended at the cemetery, which was always a stop on their walks. But this field, full of stones and humps of grass was also full of sun, and the inhabitants had the good manners to stay where they were.

"Isn't Winston a beautiful man – beautiful in his great knowledge and wisdom." began Aunt Dot. "We have known each other for a few years. There's a Shakespeare festival in two weeks, wouldn't it be fun to go? Winston invited me to attend a play this spring when his wife was visiting friends in Portland. *Pygmalion* was the play, by Shaw."

Pig, he thought to himself that makes sense, remembering the floating naked baby pig. But David White's Aunt neither required nor allowed for a response as she skipped along.
"What would you like for dinner?" she suddenly asked.

As a waif who ate at someone else's house two or three times a week he'd never been asked what he wanted for dinner. Aunt Dot didn't wait for an answer – she just struck a bee line through campus, up one block on Main, then two blocks to Spring Street. The grocery store was small yet ample. Jammed on shelves were all of the necessities. At the end of the long narrow store was a meat case and John.

"Hey, Dot, how are you today?" called John from the butcher block.
"Just fine, John, and you?"
"I'm good, what can I get you today?"
"Oh, I don't know, dear, I'm not sure what I'm in the mood for."
"What do you think, dear?" David's Aunt asked, gazing in his direction.
After a second or two David White firmly said, "Not pig."

They both laughed and decided on steak. Two small steaks were produced. Aunt Dot bought beets with the greens attached and one potato. "I don't care for potatoes, dear" informed his Aunt, "but you do."

After dinner, she taught him to play rummy, and then led him to the bookcase to pick out a book. "We'll visit the library, tomorrow. Wasn't Winston nice?" No, David thought, but he didn't dare say anything for he had nowhere else to go. It was here with Aunt Dot or nothing. At bed time his Aunt said, "Good night, David, sleep well, dear."

That night, David was tossed and rocked in a sea of formaldehyde, then awoke with a start and realized his Aunt was creaking along the pictures. He also realized he needed to use the bathroom desperately. Dot slowly climbed the stairs. David relieved himself but had a difficult time falling back to sleep. The odor of formaldehyde remained in his nose till dawn.

The yellow Ford coupe was quite fun. The seats were leather; it had a key to unlock the steering, and a button starter. Best of all was the automatic transmission. It would help when David learned to drive. The breeze blowing in his nostrils cleansed the formaldehyde from his nose and inserted within him the first slice of possibility – the first glimpse that his life could be different, better, and his. They were on their way past "Cook's Corner" to Harpswell and Bailey Island way to Lester Getchall's house on the water. Lester was a lobsterman; inherited the business from his father who drowned one winter's afternoon right off his own dock. His toe got caught on a boat cleat, hit his head on a rock and lay face down in the water until his wife found him, after calling him in for supper.

At twelve, David liked Lester; tall, burley, red flannel and rubber boots, he was hale, hardy and well met. "HULLOOO Dot." he'd always call when they drove down his drive. The food was great, lobster of course, in every way possible. Lester taught David to pitch horse shoes. Dot's eyes caught the light off the kerosene lantern in the center of the table – she liked him too. He was younger than Dot but neither seemed to mind. Lester's mother did.

She kept making excuses for him to help her in the kitchen or in the garden. It was clear that Lester had entered a lifelong contract to take care of his mother, and nothing and no one could break it. The exhilarating ride in the convertible which served his first taste of freedom remained in his nostrils but didn't linger. His very life, his shelter and food, clothes and warmth came from Dot. He espied his Aunt and Lester kissing in the boat house one time, when he was half way down the steps to the water. Looking up to the house David saw Mrs. Getchall glaring from the kitchen. David was about to turn 15 when this occurred. The ride home was silent. The walk afterward was devoid of conversation until they reached the cemetery.

"Lester's mother doesn't want me to come around anymore. She says, if she lost Lester, she wouldn't know what she would do. She was particularly pointed and the look on Lester's face told me everything."

David's first thought was how could anyone throw away a chance like that with a woman like Dorothy Tebbits? Usually his Aunt didn't allow for, nor require a response; but this time she paused and he realized he needed to say something, so he blurted out this lame and trite line: "You'll always have me." The look on her face was difficult to read – one of gratitude mixed with pity, sorrow, and determination. He felt his stomach twist a bit as an unseen string looped itself around him and knotted the line to Aunt Dot when she responded, "Yes dear I hope I will."

After three years with David, Dot began to think of this companion as a constant companion. She would never have a child and David White was growing into a man. He was slim but tall and possessed a sensitive and grateful heart. Theirs was not an aunt and nephew relationship nor a mother and son link – perhaps more symbiotic.

The pair visited Winston, again. Disturbed by those jars, David's habit was to wait outside. That was fine with his Aunt so sometimes he would walk to the library and read. He could read the books even though he wasn't a student and David liked to read. His Aunt Dot would find him and the pair would continue the walk. David White had his own thoughts to keep him company anyway: Stephanie Johnston.

David White was a sophomore in high school and there was a new girl from Nova Scotia. She was an athlete, trim, lithe, and supple. Fiddling with his locker between classes he waited for a glimpse. It was her thighs that he loved best – tanned, firm from swimming and running. Of course skirts below the knee didn't allow for much of a look, but imagination provided a better image than reality. She swished past him and he said, "Hi, Stephanie. How are you? So glad you came to the U.S. and are attending my high school. Why don't you come over for dinner tonight? My Aunt is making lobster and corn on the cob. Then maybe we could take a walk to Bowdoin and I can show you the library where I study."

He said nothing of the kind. A shy and sensitive boy from a backwoods town like Penobscot Mills was much more adept at speaking with his Aunt's adult friends than kids his own age. That had been the sum of his life thus far in Brunswick so David White simply said, "Hi."

Stephanie said, "Hello," and smiled an inviting smile, full of truth, directness, and possibility. He froze. There was no chronometer anyone could employ to measure the length of time he stared at her – a second or two really, but it was an excruciating prison sentence from which he was blessedly pardoned by two girls who came and invited her to eat lunch with them. What a dope! It would take until his senior year before he conversed in anything resembling an easy manner.

Not so with Evan Newell. Dot and David met him at an art fair. He was one of the artists and the three of them became fast friends. He lived on a point overlooking the ocean with a grand view from his living room and a baby grand piano as well. He played, joked, and made martinis. Dot was unschooled in the ways of the drink but Evan was so cultured that she eased into his life style with the broadest smile she had ever employed. Evan had money of his own so the pair with Evan began frequenting The Seven Seas Restaurant – a small, dark, carpeted room with a bar and lounge area. Bed time began to stretch. Evan even convinced Dot to let David have one glass of beer. These were small glasses, and when you knew the owner and bartender, Ronnie Polk, no one thought anything of it. David was almost eighteen by then anyway.

Back home David asked his Aunt if she played the piano in the living room. She simply said, "We don't play that piano, dear." The tone hinted of a secret as to why the piano remained silent. Dot knew that the songs of the heart were far too dangerous. For years she pursued one man then another – always in a demure respectable manner and always with a close grip on her guard. In fact the piano went silent the day

Dot's parents died in their bed upstairs. The bodies remained for almost three days before Dot called to report their death.

It was with Evan that Dot first touched anyone, or anyone touched her, except for that kissing thing with Lester. Evan had his arm around her often, rubbed her back, and stroked her cheek. He'd slap David on the shoulder too and give him a little fake jab to the jaw. But Dorothy Tebbits was different with Evan than she had been with anyone. Before her parents died she had a meager social life and after, she withdrew and watched – in fact she was a virgin.

Winston Douglas touched her bottom once and she recoiled as if she had been bitten by one of the stuffed snakes on the shelf. The strong arms of Lester Getchal convinced Dot to allow a kiss but it was easy for her to leave Lester when his mother told her to. David became a safe young man and was a fantasy partner. Evan Newell was quite different. They went away for a weekend once. Though it was fun and they were together all forty two hours, Dorothy Tebbits returned a virgin.

The weekend Dot and Evan went to Boston was strange. Since his Aunt Dot's care, love, security and partnership, David White had never been alone in the house and sounds, odors and uncertain breezes began to enter his awareness. "Hello," He said one night. No answer, so he peeked into the kitchen to find everything as it should be. He took a deep breath and a very faint odor of formaldehyde filled his senses. It stung his nostrils and sickened his stomach the way it did years before with Professor Douglas. Imagination is a great tool for a thoughtful sensitive fellow who would endeavor to become a writer, but left unchecked it conjures much. David lay in his bed, his eyes squeezed tight until dawn and ignored imagined foot falls and taps.

David's first semester of his senior year, he began conversing with Stephanie. He ran track (long distance) and they had sports in common since she was a swimmer. David mentioned this fact to Evan and to his surprise when Dot came to pick him up after school; Evan was in the front seat and Stephanie in the back. It had been worked out so they went to The Seven Seas for dinner. Sitting next to Stephanie in the back seat of the coupe, their thighs almost touching, David could smell sweet powder on her and could barely breathe.

Soon after, they were having dinner at Evan's house. Evan and David were sitting on the sofa looking out at the ocean and remembering the time swimming in the cove. The water turned their ankles blue then, so they couldn't imagine how cold it was now. Evan put his left arm around David's shoulder and remained silent. David White regarded Evan as the father he never had – as someone who could teach him how to be a man. Then Evan Newell put his right hand on David's thigh. This was new information. David stiffened. "David, it's time for us to leave," commanded Dot from behind them. David, in a slight state of confusion, stood, grabbed his coat and exited. Dot started the car and drove.

"Sorry, David, that was not right for Evan to do. You'll be ok though, no harm done, but we won't be seeing him anymore. Give your little friend, Stephanie a call when we get home, why don't you." There it was that calm assurance, the same as when he saw the floating baby pig. He knew he would be alright but didn't feel like calling Stephanie. Dot turned to him with a familiar look of pity, sorrow, and determination. Dot knew they would return to Professor Winston Douglas. David hoped that would be the case since the strings knotting him to Dorothy Tebbits, his protector, benefactor, and surrogate paramour were cinching closer.

A couple of weeks later, David was studying in the Bowdoin library and couldn't concentrate. Dot was at the biology building. David wanted to go home, so he crossed the distance to the biology building quickly. It was cold, snowy, and windy. Stepping down the half flight and into the hall he heard voices.

"Don't you understand? I don't want you coming around anymore. There has never been anything between us; I don't love you. You've become a pest, a nag, and a hag." The door swung open and Dot squirted through the door in short quick steps. Her head was down, hands clasped together and wringing until her knuckles were red. She swept past David, up the steps and straight home.

From that moment on she didn't leave the house. She slept during the day and became a sentry through the night, tapping the photographs, sometimes so loudly David thought they would fall off the wall. He began bringing trays to her, in her room. She didn't eat much.

This was actually the first time he had been in her room since he had arrived. There were two bedrooms upstairs – one was Dot's and the other a shrine for grandmother and grandfather. Entering Dot's bedroom for the first time, David had a dreadful feeling similar to the biology lab. Dorothy Tebbits had a collection of dolls, maybe a couple hundred, all trapped behind glass cases and seeing them, he shivered. He knew then that he couldn't leave her. David White had never established friends in Brunswick, Penobscot Mills was years behind and his best friend there was a retarded girl who had been murdered. David then understood something of what Lester Getchall must have felt for his mother. He stopped attending school and when they called, he said that his Aunt was ill and he needed to take care of her. Stephanie called once in the spring to ask if he would be attending the University of Maine next fall. She was enrolled. David could only say he couldn't but might next term. He never did. David was eighteen then. He found himself at twenty three; still with Dot at the house, drinking his formaldehyde and watching.

The grist for each day was milled slowly – a trip to see John at the grocery, to the fish monger twice a week, a tray at breakfast, one at noon and another at 5:30. Dot ate little and talked less. David read everything in the house and visited the public library for more. Crossword puzzles in the *Brunswick Times Record* or the *Portland Press Herald* were digested each day. Yard work was accomplished and snow shoveled. David saw Stephanie once later the next year. He took a day and drove to the University of Maine and located her from the one letter he had received which named the sorority in which she lived. David White sauntered on a foreign campus to the sorority house. He was not certain if he had the nerve to meet her. She was sitting on the porch right next to a fellow he recognized from Penobscot Mills; they talked and were holding hands. They didn't see him.

It was after dinner when he returned. Dot was downstairs standing by the piano. She turned when he entered and said, "Please, dear, don't do that again. I paced all day and now I'm tired and have to go to bed. You can bring me a tray if you like."

David found himself awake in the middle of the night, standing in front of the black and whites. Tears came quickly and he began to sob and heave great breaths of sorrow at those pictures. Dot appeared and placed her hands on his shoulders. "What's the matter, David?"

He uttered nothing, for he had no words to describe hopeless desolation – suffocated at the thought that he was becoming his Aunt. He was tending the invalid, unable to emotionally break from a woman who had saved him – been so much to him. She held David, and that was odd for she'd never done so before. She went back to bed.

Dorothy Tebbits did not sleep that night. Smelling an acrid odor she crossed to her parent's vacant bedroom. The impressions of their bodies outlined in vivid detail every movement. Indeed she was sure she saw the bed crumple and heard the creak of very old maple. She had made David a warden in the same way she had accepted that task years before. She loved him in perhaps an inappropriate way and wept at what she had done.

The telephone rang one night and David reached for it with a start. There was no one on the line. He felt a hand on his shoulder, jumped and turned. Nobody was there. A few nights went by and he awoke to the sound of Dot talking. She was whispering on the phone to someone. He didn't intrude and simply waited for her to make her rounds and go back up stairs.

He came to predict his Aunt's nightly rounds and often awoke just as she stepped to the piano. Cracking his eyes slowly, he noticed the she was dressed in fancy clothes and was carrying a pocketbook. She tapped several photographs, took Evan Newell's photo off the wall revealing an unsoiled square. She walked quietly out of the room, through the kitchen and silently out the side door. David spied her as she walked down the drive to the tar sidewalk then turn toward the grove of pine. Not wishing to intrude he crept slowly out the same door and paced to the front lawn. She achieved the corner as if floating and he thought he might be dreaming. A black sedan slowed and stopped. She turned and smiled for she knew he was following. Dorothy Tebbits threw a quick, vigorous wave of determination, and then the car door closed.

The street light cast her silhouette on the window, a profile as still and emotionless as those in formaldehyde jars. She was gone.

David stood for minutes in his pajamas then turned to the house. He felt certain that his imagination was turning over and over again like the starter of the yellow coupe. The upstairs windows were filling with formaldehyde, cloudy and yellow. Shapes materialized. There was definite light and people moving back and forth. The fear forbade his feet to move. The grove of pine whispered and something akin to dread entered his stomach. Tending Dot the rest of his life would have been a desolate existence. Being abandoned once again was terrifying. David White forced himself to walk through the door. A cold breath struck his face then from around the corner poked one head, then another from the piano. He fell into a chair in the kitchen and watched black and white figures stroll, silently passed him. There was mildew from each breath as they left the house.

David awoke the next morning with his head on the kitchen table. At his hand was a folder which revealed the deed to the house and title to the coupe. He never saw his Aunt Dot again. Lester hadn't seen her. Summoning the courage, David confronted Professor Douglas. No he hadn't seen her either. Ronnie Polk at The Seven Seas said he hadn't seen her. "What about Evan Newell?" David asked. "Don't know," he replied, "but his house is all closed up." In about a month David received a picture post card from Rome and in a happy scrawl she said, "Having a wonderful time!" He began to receive one card a month from various parts of the world.

Dorothy Tebbits made a determined choice in her parent's bedroom that night when sounds, shadows, and impressions on bed linen revealed to her what she had done those past

5 years. David had become her caretaker and martyr. The conversation with Evan Newell was difficult at first but soon the pair realized a new form of symbiosis could serve them. Dot the stable yet adventuresome companion and Evan the cultured, well off artist would travel – Evan choosing one male after another and Dot enjoying life out in the world.

David White tends bar at The Seven Seas and is taking classes at Bowdoin College in English Literature. He thinks he might become a writer. This is the only story he knows so far. There is more activity at the house and he's had a few friends over and spent a weekend in Bar Harbor. The piano remains silent, however, and David White has hung a black and white photograph of Stephanie on the wall.

# TREE TOPS

Rutherford Nesbit escaped to the top of a tree whenever he could. Hugging cold black trunks, he'd scooch one armful at a time until the first limb was reached; then daring, he inhabited the highest branch that was willing to support him. Swaying, he rode the breeze like sailing a small sloop. No one could touch him there. He rode for a few more minutes atop his friend, but it was growing dark and time to head home.

Crossing but a few streets from the forest he walked into his tiny house. He entered the kitchen to find a bowl, spoon and napkin set as he had left them. An empty sauce pan sat on the electric stove top and a can of tomato soup kept it company. Nine oyster crackers had been meted out and the can opener was at hand. It was always thus here on earth for Rutherford Nesbit. An ordered life was a predictable life. He awoke before dawn, had a quick breakfast of shredded wheat, washed the bowl and spoon then walked to work. He needed to arrive before anyone else was around.

He was employed as the pay master at the Penobscot Paper Mill – a sprawling complex that hugged the river from which it gathered logs that had been floated down stream. It ate the logs and spat out paper.

This habit of riding tree tops began in his mid teens. He stared through the chain link fence at a basketball game, grasping galvanized wire with slender pink fingers. His thoughts drifted at the rustle of leaves from a white oak at the edge of the town park. The swirling leaves reached for him and begged a favor. WAM! A basketball struck the fence and crushed his fingers. The boy, who threw the ball laughed, saying, "Wake up Frankie." He retrieved his fingers, held his arms straight to his sides without swinging them and walked away in his usual stilted fashion. The nick name 'Frankie' was due to his Frankenstein walk. The boys returned to the game as he reached the white oak. He was soon at the top, out of sight and riding his first real friend.

He named only one tree, even though he knew all of them and they knew him. He called the white oak in the park, 'Gladys.' Her pale gray and scaly bark had fissured with age and stood nearly 100 feet tall. Her species was *quercus alba* and was the state tree of Connecticut, Illinois, and Maryland. He knew the Latin names of all his friends. He referred to the white oak as a she, even though both male and female flowers are born on the same plant, as it is with many trees.

Climbing required strong thighs and arms which he did not possess at first, but the need to ride became an obsession, so he grew over the years. This did nothing to help his stilted walk, but being the paymaster at the mill, no one called him Frankie anymore. He was Mr. Nesbit.

His second tree was an American Beech, species *fagus grandifolia,* and the nuts were delicious. This one stood a full 120 feet tall and provided a vista unmatched by other trees in town. Its bark was gray and smooth which was easier on his thighs and arms. Once at the top, he'd grasp a handful of branch in each hand and let the wind sway him back and forth. Over the years he came to know which branches were willing to support him – not able to support his weight, but willing. They wanted him to ride as much as he did.

The 'sisters' were both maple – one silver, *acer saccharinum* and one sugar, *acer saccharum*. He rode many maples throughout the town and nearby forest, but when he encountered either maple type he always uttered, "Your sister says, hi." These were somewhat easier to climb since the first limbs were often lower to the ground. The tops were more alive than some other, sturdier trees and he rode them with glee. He learned to place one foot on a limb while grasping a handful of leaves, then place the other foot about three feet away on another limb and grasp that handful of leaves. He'd rock like that for many hours even when there was no breeze. It was a sugar maple who got him to change his breakfast routine – pancakes now and real maple syrup. On earth he did not vary much about his life and he always ate only two pancakes with one eighth cup of syrup.

The white spruce was quite a tree; 100 feet tall with branches evenly spaced, finished in a cone of solace. *Picea glauca* held his senses unlike deciduous trees. The scent was overwhelming and grasping the tip with both hands; he'd ride – swinging to and fro until he thought he would faint. Black spruce, *picea mariana*, were less plentiful than the white and grew in higher elevations usually, but held the same sensual fascination.

He didn't really have a favorite tree, but white pines, *pinus strobus*, standing 153 feet tall, ramrod straight and loyal were hypnotic. Except for the sap as with any other evergreen, they were easy to climb and had the same advantage as maples. The tops were alive, even more so than the maples, and they refused to break. He became most daring on white pine trees, often swinging and riding with one hand; tempting fate. There was nothing stilted in the manner in which he rode these trees. No one would ever confuse him with Frankenstein among these tree tops – no he fairly flew from limb to limb until exhausted. This was also the first and only time he fell.

He didn't fall to earth, just 9 feet or so to an accommodating branch which caught his buttocks like an easy chair and cradled his head. This was no accident he knew. After riding trees for years now, he had come to depend on a willing partnership. Still, he decided not to press his luck.

Descending the *pinus strobus*, he began thinking about the next day at work. It would be difficult for him – requiring him to speak to a group about a change in payroll deductions. He would rather fall to earth from 100 feet than face people.

Rutherford Nesbit arrived at work the next day in the dark. He turned the light on in his office and surveyed the scene. The cleaning crew had obeyed his orders and left his office alone. He'd clean as needed and he didn't want anyone molesting his things. The desk held a copy of his presentation which was to take place at 10:00 in the morning, over four hours from now. He liked getting to work early for two desperate reasons: he could get off work early enough to ride his trees and he didn't know how to talk to people. Most of the office employees did not come in until 9:00. When his boss came in, Rutherford went directly to him and said, "I don't want to do this today, OK?" He turned to leave and Joe Pittman called him back. "Rutherford, you're the only one who can explain this. It will take only 10 minutes or so and I'll be there but you have to do this." Rutherford stared at Joe without emotion for several seconds, then turned and exited quickly.

Entering his office he was quite certain he had forgotten how to breathe. How could this have happened? He learned to breathe nearly forty years ago and had been doing it ever since. How do you forget something like that? He opened his mouth but nothing came in or went out of it. Leaning his hands on his desk he forced air out of his lungs and gasped in a loud yelping noise until he calmed himself. He would simply read his copy of the changes the employees would find on their pay stubs next week. They each would have a copy. It would be alright he said to himself. He went to the bathroom five times in the hour. It was 10:00 and he entered a small conference room where 16 managers and foremen sat or stood.

Mr. Nesbit began to read, not looking up from his text until he finished in record time; six minutes, forty three seconds. He was done – finished, it was over. Elevating his eyes he noticed a hand in the air, swaying gently; fingers flopping – limp and uninspired. He would never ride such a tree as that, he thought. That tree was not his friend – not one upon which he could count – not one who would catch him if he fell.

"Mr. Nesbit. This doesn't say anything about the hourly employees. Are they affected as well?" said the owner of the limp and untrustworthy tree.

He was not prepared for this; no Q and A for heaven's sake. He leaned on the lectern, reminding himself of what he had learned an hour earlier about breathing. He was smart and he could do this. "No because of the union contract, hourly workers are not affected. Your pension is totally separate."

Great, it's over he thought and now time to leave. Then he beheld a forest before him. A half dozen or so trees sprouted across the room – some oaks, some pine, at least one beech that he could see. What was he to do? His eyes became glassy; then suddenly he saw these hands, not as questions to be feared but trees to be ridden. He pointed to the beech and responded to the question; then to a white pine; then an oak and a couple of maples until all trees had withdrawn and the room was silent. Rutherford Nesbit looked at Joe Pittman and escaped the conference room to his office. It took the rest of the day for Rutherford to learn what actually happened during that presentation.

"Hey, Nesbit, good job buddy, didn't know I was a maple tree and what's with this, *acer saccharum*?" said one manager.

"Ya, I know, I'm an oak. Always knew I was the strong silent type." said the night foreman. "What was it, *quercus alba*? Cool."

Even the office staff was talking about it with faint admiration for Rutherford's arboreal knowledge, or perhaps his humor.

"Humor?" thought Rutherford. I wasn't trying to be funny. He began to realize that he had been calling the managers and foremen by his tree names complete with the Latin species. "Oh dear," Rutherford said to himself. He would be the laughing stock of the mill. As the day wore on, he realized that this was not the case. The joking was good humored and there was an admiration in the looks and comments he got. For the first time in years, perhaps in his life, people actually saw HIM. He had been invisible most of his life.

After work he paced quickly to 'Gladys' and rode her, recalling his day. She seemed glad for him and responded with a little extra grace. "Ah, kinesis, the feeling of motion," Rutherford thought, what a marvelous and heady feeling – to be flying through the sky, tethered lightly by a deep and abiding friend. He sailed great arcs around her tops – far more than he had the first time years ago. Sitting for a moment, straddling a limb and riding as one might a child's stick horse, Rutherford Nesbit began to find the courage to admit something. There was a small guilt behind his belly button that made him wince at the thought that he worked for the beast that ate logs and spat out paper. Those bodies floating down river were once fiends. He sighed. But having people 'see' him today was nice. He found a longing fill his chest – a longing for a mate, a partner, someone to love.

When he returned to work the next day, he was invisible once again. But the longing for someone to love remained. Speaking to females, however, only produced nights of echoing terror. He regretted every encounter. Recalling the 'fun' everyone demonstrated yesterday at his tree naming, he approached a woman in the office whom he thought was pretty. Without introduction he blundered, "You are a weeping willow, *salix babylonica*." Rutherford stood there grinning. He did not possess a natural smile, for his eyes reflected the memory of terror from nights of regret long ago.

All the woman heard was: "You are sex and Babylon" and was mortified. Rutherford retreated. He decided to take his first vacation in years. A week riding his friends through the forest would improve his mood.

Saturday morning, he packed some food for the day and walked directly to the forest. He selected a beech tree about three hundred yards from the road. Dropping his pack, he ascended the beech and began swinging. The day was glorious and he rocked slowly letting the memories of the past week float away. He had gone directly to Joe Pittman and explained the reference to the weeping willow and Joe suggested that he stop the tree talk. With each sway he regained a robust confidence and returned to the true joy of riding his friend – to the thrill each movement brought just as he reached the nadir of an arc. That was the point at which he could almost fall, but instead bound back to the zenith of his arc and reach the apogee – the residence of weightlessness, which he gleefully inhabited over and over again.

Slowing, he took the opportunity of riding the tallest tree around, to search for others he might inhabit. Looking toward the Northwest he espied a stand of tall pine. Judging them to be approximately three miles away, he claimed his desire.

Once on earth he grabbed his pack and struck off toward new adventure.

He was warm when he reached the stand of pine and found them to be *picea mariana*, black spruce. When he reached the cone of solace, he removed his shirt. The freedom he felt was exhilarating. He began swinging wildly with much abandon. He intended to enjoy all he could this week. At the nadir of one of his arcs he felt a perceptible shove, and upon reaching the zenith, expecting to become weightless, he instead was launched off the tree to land on another. He landed well for he knew how to use his feet and strong arms. There was no fear and looking back to the tree who launched him thus, she was shaking with laughter. Rutherford began to laugh as well, then he did what she knew he would. He swung back and was again launched, this time to a different tree. The landing was a little more difficult due to his shoes. He removed them and his socks and flew to another tree. Soon he was flying from tree to tree, shirtless and shoeless, and laughing continuously.

He returned to earth and collected his pack, brought it to the top and rested while he ate. Rutherford looked toward where he supposed town to be. He could just glimpse the smoke stacks of the mill. He knew; of course he knew, when it grew dark, he would simply leap home with the help of all of his friends. And that's just what he did.

Over the next weeks, well into September and early October, Rutherford leapt through the forest across the leafy canopy of his friends. He ventured further into the depths of dark green pine needles and waxy broad leaves until he could only guess where the town was. He traveled shirtless and barefoot with a small pack strapped to his back. His sense of direction came from dead reckoning with a fixed point in space – Mount Katahdin, the tallest peak in the Appalachian range, standing one mile high. He knew he could not reach it in a weekend so it would have to wait for a vacation, but he didn't feel like taking a vacation without someone else. He had begun to yearn for the company of a female. He thought about this often when he paused and rocked gently, soaking in the sun.

On his travels he saw the scars of logging and thought about his occupation at the paper mill. He was not particularly ashamed because he needed to make a living – no one else was going to take care of him – but he felt conflicted.

Autumn was as hand, the weather turning with the leaves and riding his friends would have to be postponed until spring could open her eyes again and entice the summer to return. Northeastern climate limited riding trees in winter to a few sunny times atop a white pine, wearing a bright red parka. Winter was difficult for Rutherford Nesbit; a lonely time, and so he waited.

The eyelids of spring did open, a bit earlier than usual and Rutherford took full advantage of a favorable weather report the first week in May by taking a short vacation. Ascending the tall beech out of town, Rutherford vaulted toward the mountain. Tree after tree accepted his desire and cheered him on toward Mount Katahdin. Resting, rocking, in sight of the still snowy peak, Rutherford Nesbit nearly fell as he beheld a face in the nearest tree.

Grasping the cone of solace from a black spruce was a man who was as startled to see Rutherford as he was. Unlike on earth, Rutherford was quite in his element atop a very tall beech and simply smiled and greeted the stranger.

"Hello there. Beautiful day, don't you think?" said Rutherford.

"Yes, I agree especially for early May." replied the stranger.
Then the stranger asked, "Are you alone?"

"Yes sir I am, and you?" Rutherford strongly responded.

"No," said the stranger, "I travel with my three friends here."

Sure enough, Rutherford saw three others riding the nearest trees. On one of them was a girl. Her name was Audrey. She had auburn red hair, deep blue eyes, skin the color of the clouds that framed her face and she was barefoot. Shirtless and barefoot, Rutherford smiled a becoming smiled and asked her name. Others were introduced. Jeffrey was the first stranger he met, Dennis, the second, Mitchell the third and then Audrey.

They all quickly showed their skill at vaulting themselves (with the help of their friends the trees) across the forest ceiling and began frolicking among the black spruce and white pine. Rutherford engineered an occasion to ride the top of the same tree as Audrey. "Raise your hand," said Rutherford. She did with a coy smile. Rutherford said, "You are an *acer saccharum*."

"Sugar Maple," Audrey interrupted with delight. Examining her hand and arm she agreed. "Hold up your hand, Rutherford. You are a *fagus grandifolia*." and Rutherford gleefully said, "Beech!"

Thrilled to be likened to such a tall, stately tree, he grasped Audrey's hand and kissed it. Rutherford became aware that his ease at talking with Audrey was most unlike his behavior on earth.

"Where are you all from," Rutherford asked.
"The town," was the collective reply.

"The town, but how could this be? I live in town and I've never seen any of you. Have you ever seen me," asked Rutherford?

Summoning a pitiful countenance, Jeffrey explained, "We are all invisible on earth. I didn't know Dennis, Mitchell or Audrey in town. We just happened to meet here, in the forest, as we did you."

"What is your job in town," asked Dennis?

"I'm the pay master for the mill," replied Rutherford.

"You're Mr. Nesbit; the person who signs my pay check?" blurted Dennis.

"I must have passed you a dozen times in the hall. Mitchell works at the bank and Jeffrey is at the post office."

Rutherford turned to Audrey who said, "Bookstore."

"Why I probably bought my tree book from you and didn't even know it," said Rutherford, shaking his head.

They slept that night on tree tops – Rutherford and Audrey in the same white pine. Reclining on the adjacent branch he heard her breathe all night – making sweet squeaking sounds. Her face, in repose, caught the moon and kept it captive – her brows pressing at each other revealed a dream and her lips parted in a silent smile of joy. Yes Rutherford was falling in love and he felt the same heady kinesis of vacillating from nadir to zenith from every tree he'd ever ridden.

Upon returning to town, Rutherford realized that he had changed – he no longer walked in a stilted fashion but with a swagger that bespoke confidence. The five faded into the town at twilight – the end of a thrilling week. The next morning, Rutherford changed his route to work and stopped by the bookstore. He gazed into the darkened shop and was overcome with the happy nadir and zenith of his life – the depths and peaks that defined him – Audrey, the girl he'd just met. He imagined her shelving books as she must have done countless times, and he smiled.

At work, Rutherford strolled through the outer office and talked with the clerks a little. He sauntered through the plant, looking for Dennis and found him in the finishing room, where paper was being wound on huge rolls. They chatted for a bit, or rather yelled, for it was very noisy there. After work he stopped by the book store again and boldly walked in.

"Hello," he said to a woman he presumed to be the owner. "Is Audrey here?"

"Yes," she replied, "In the back." She gestured toward the rear of the shop where oversized books and atlases were shelved.

Rutherford realized he was nervous, but not in the same way he'd been all his life. No, he was excited to see Audrey again. Gliding straight to the back, he saw her, crouched down at a lower shelf. Dressed in conservative slacks and blouse, her hair tied in a bun, she looked small and delicate He said, "Good afternoon, Audrey."

Her smile was immediate. It would have been clear to anyone watching how much Audrey was pleased to see him, but no one gave any notice. They stared at each other for a while, not because of shyness or a lack of conversation, but for the sheer joy of being in each other's presence.

"Please come to dinner tonight," invited Rutherford. "It may be bachelor's food, but I make a good pot roast." She gladly accepted. That night spun on and on through the sharing of two life stories until they both knew it was time to leave. Rutherford walked Audrey home and standing at her door, he suddenly realized, he really didn't know what to do. Audrey rescued him by standing on tip toes and grasping the back of his neck, pressed her lips to his. The kiss was brief, but Rutherford couldn't remember how he got home.

For the next weeks, well into June and July they met in town, shared sandwiches upon the trees and swung together through the forest. They adopted the habit of eating lunch on Saturdays at a small café. It was here where they began to interact with others in the town. A stout woman who worked at the library noticed the tree book that Rutherford and Audrey were studying and asked, "You interested in trees, are you?"

"Why yes," replied Audrey, "especially the tall ones."
"Why especially the tall ones?" queried the librarian.
"We actually like to climb them and swing from their tops," explained Rutherford. "It takes a sizable tree to do that. We call it riding the tree."
Fascinated, the librarian sought more details. Slowly the people on earth began to see Audrey and Rutherford as perhaps a little kooky, but always fascinating. "How strong do you have to be?" "What's it like." "What can you see?" The questions kept coming on Saturday mornings at the café.

One night as Rutherford was walking Audrey home, she commented that they both had begun to enjoy people a little bit more than ever in their lives. Rutherford turned to Audrey and said, "I would never have had the courage without you. Holding hands in the café and discussing trees with others is still scary, but you're right, I am more comfortable."

Fairly deep in the forest one day they swayed along together like two gazelles, bounding over the savannah. Rutherford was shirtless and shoeless as usual and Audrey griped the branches with her bare toes. Rocking softly next to Rutherford she parted her lips in another coy smile. Fixing his eyes to hers, she unbuttoned her blouse, removed it and her bra – and then bounded away with great abandon.

Rutherford chased her for what seemed like hours. When they stopped they made love. They didn't have sex. No that would wait until they could be married – they simply held each other, letting the wrapping of leaf and limb express all they felt.

In two weeks, the beginning of August, they were married atop a white pine. A black spruce gave the blessing, Jeffrey, Dennis and Mitchell were the best men and the sister maples were the bridesmaids. Audrey moved in to Rutherford's house and took the name of Nesbit. They both found a love of cooking and shared chores easily. Work became only time away from each other, time to long and dream.

Audrey suggested that they take a vacation down south. She wanted to learn to make real southern style biscuits and they both would ride, *taxodium distichum*, the bald cypress. It was the first time either had left town in a car. The pendulum of time swung so rapidly when he was with Audrey, it was if the clocks were riding trees post haste to reach infinity. All too soon they had to return to the paper mill town that was their home.

All the way home an undefined worry rested in both of them. This was not just because the vacation was at an end. Something else pulled their thoughts askew. Upon returning they knew. Striking directly for the park Rutherford and Audrey Nesbit stood in reverent silence at Gladys' stump. She was laid out to her full 87 feet on the earth, still, motionless. Gladys could no longer dance. There was no grace in her limbs. Audrey looked at Rutherford. They heard the logs at the mill fall to earth from the conveyor and be loaded into the barker. They could not take part in this any longer – Rutherford working in the beast that ate logs and spat out paper and Audrey in the book store – a graveyard of their friends.

The Tree Top Café can be found next to the drug store and is open for breakfast and lunch. Rutherford and Audrey need the afternoons to ride their trees. Few if any paper products are used save for the table and chairs. Pancakes or crepes, biscuits and muffins with generous sides of bacon and sausage are found on the menu. Maple syrup, blueberries, walnuts and pecans, even beech nuts can be had at the Tree Top Café. The café contains small trees and plants arranged throughout. Inhabiting an old warehouse, Rutherford and Audrey built nine levels and landings for the diners. The walls, landings, steps and lofts were festooned with paintings of lush green vines.

People come as regulars and visitors to see and talk with the couple who ride trees. The café is always busy and filled with laughter. No service is required since customers order and picked up food on the first level. This allows Audrey and Rutherford to cook together and greet their customers.

"Hey, Rutherford, what am I," said two women holding up their hands.
"Sister maples," smiled Rutherford.

There were many hands raised in the months to come – so many that the tree book was well worn. Trees that were not found in the northeastern forest were represented in the growing clientele and the 'tree couple' became quite expert.

A crowd gathered in front of the darkened Tree Top Café. A man stepped to the door. You know me, Mitchell from the bank. Rutherford and Audrey asked me to tack this notice on the door of the Tree Top Café. Rutherford and Audrey will be gone for at least a month. They're out west somewhere. They said they wanted to ride *pinus latifolia*, the lodge pole pine. And of course try their hands and feet on *sequoiadendron giganteum*, the giant sequoia standing 260 feet tall. But they'll be back.

# THE WEATHER REPORT

When I cup my hands from ear to mouth and whisper, I can say anything I want and no one can hear me – but I can hear me. *"Hello, babble—babble, what, what, secret… What's the weather report? Got to have the weather. Come on weather channel…stupid T.V.…no it's not going to be sunny…sunny—sunny. Oh, only I can hear me now. Stop this, stop this."*

Lower your hands and look around the room. Breathe and listen. Ok, I'm better. It can't be good for me to live inside my head like this but where else am I going to live? The clock says 3:35. No the clock doesn't *say* anything I know but it's only 3:35 in the afternoon. Better than 3:35 in the morning – that's the witching hour, not midnight. That's the cold sweat time. Desolation oozes out in drops of horror. Just wait, it will be alright. It will be alright at 4:30.

He said I could call after 4:30 today. Why does it take so long? I've been waiting all day, why am I worked up now – one hour before I can call? Pace, yes let's pace – living room, down the hall into the bedroom, turn around and walk. Let's do this five times. Ok that's one – again, now two and three and faster this time, four now five.

Is the weather on? What time is it? 3:39? What if he says no? Oh that can't happen. Ok sit now. Finger tips to finger tips, my right palm at my mouth and my left palm extended at my left ear I can say *"anything."* *"What do I want to say? What's the weather? Raining right now – sheets and sheets – whisper, whisper. I'm glad I'm alone right now – wife and kids gone to her mother's. It will be alright at 4:30. But what if the answer's no? I can hear me, can you hear me?"*

Stop it!

Ok, sit and relax. Look around the room. That's a handsome bookcase. I've always thought so – tall slim, dark wood and porcelain knobs. Reaching nearly to the ceiling, it stands and looks at me. Her eyes are the rounded facade of the highest shelf. It's not my fault. I have to tell myself, "It's not my fault." She's looking down her nose at me. I could have made you, you know. Besides a carpenter I'm a cabinet maker. Have to keep reminding myself of my worth. It's not my fault.

What's the time? 3:43? Pace some more. How many times? Let's do seven this time. Up the hall to the bedroom then down again into the kitchen, around the table and back up again. Once…now that's two times. Faster, move the clock ahead. Three, then four – huffing and puffing now – too much stress. Now five times, six, and seven. Time? 3:44. Damn! Sit!

I shouldn't have started that business. What was I thinking? Yes I worked hard and I'm a skilled carpenter but went belly up – bankruptcy, debt, and now the house – oh damn the house. Three months behind, no food in the house. What are my babies and wife going to eat when they come back? Can't let them see me like this but I can't hold on. That last guy shouldn't have backed out. I could have built that house. He has the money, he's just cheap – and scared I guess. Well so am I, damn it!

Rub my hand over the brocade of the sofa – somewhat worn but still ok. Stroke, stroke slow and steady. Maybe I can hypnotize myself so I won't hurt. Lay down now. I can feel myself bleed into my stomach. Like I've been gut shot – I bleed and ooze warm deep wrenching pain. Still pouring sheets and sheets outside. The weather – oh I missed the weather again.

But not sunny—sunny – sunny. Maybe at 4:30. What time is it now? I can't look. 3:51.

In a small town, everybody knows you which should be a good thing. But when the crash happens, and no work, everybody knows your business. I walk by places I've built and remember the feel of wood, nails, screws, even splinters were welcome. I see that skeleton before it grew flesh – the flesh that comes from living in it – from the daily joys, sorrows, arguments. Boy my wife and I have had some blow outs recently. No more work; none for three and a half months – not since that guy backed out. Lucky I could get my money back from the lumber yard. The look in the lumberman's eyes – I can still see what he was thinking – "what a loser" his eyes said; and the smirk on this face. Believe it or not, a little pity would have been nice.

I've worked hard; I've always worked hard. Half way through college I knew what I wanted to do – what I should be doing and work was good for a few years. If you try and do your best you can't fail – bull shit! Failure is when you try your hardest, do everything right and it's no good in the end – and you're a bum. It's not my fault but who let everybody down? ME! Oh shit, my stomach hurts. I can feel the bleeding – internal bleeding.

Wife and kids due back at 5:00. It will be alright at 4:30 but what if it's not? What if it's the end, the cliff of failure and shame? A precipice – oh I wish I could jump but I don't have the courage for that – besides what would my kids think? That's a nice Tiffany style lamp – expensive I remember. Christmas present for my wife. Maybe we could sell it. Can't sell it in time for dinner though. The base is black with high shoulders like an elegant woman with a long flowing gown, her arms curved down to her sides. What time is it? 3:54.

I remember in grammar school I was always interested in how things were made. I'd walk around the inside of newly poured foundations, looking at the pipes erupting from the floor that would become the plumbing system. I still like the smell of newly poured cement – it brings me back to a happy time – one without worry. Tommy, Bobby, Paul and I would pretend the foundation was a pirate ship and we'd sail to strange lands. It was even better once the sub-floor was in and an array of two by four studs became the sails.

Tommy is at the bank now and that makes things strained. Three months behind in payments and Tommy has been patient but he can't hold out any longer. I've had to do some embarrassing things in the past year. Begging him was one. Bankruptcy was another difficult time when the business went south.

There were some good times though. I can still feel the breeze from the water when Dad and I went fishing in that stream up the mountain. The patience he took tying those multicolored flies – feathers everywhere – he really was an artist. Wish I had taken the time to learn while he was alive. The dusty ball diamond where we used to play catch has a house on it now. High school baseball felt like a success for me – the time I stole home. Really hard to do because you need a right handed hitter so the catcher can't see you. Then I had to wait until the catcher lost the ball (which happens from time to time) and run like hell.

The first job I got right out of high school was helping old Bill Mackenzie. He'd been a carpenter for thirty years or more. I liked swinging a hammer and seeing how buildings were constructed. He was a cabinet maker too and that was a challenge to learn. He left me all of his tools when he retired. I remember one time when (all by himself – I was a kid then just watching) he cut a garage in half, moved the pieces apart and propped them up, then finished the middle to make a two car garage. That was amazing!

But Tommy was going to college so I guess I thought I should too. I'm glad for one decision I made, which was to quit after two years and come back to be a carpenter. I believe I made something of myself in this small mill town. Tommy did too. Bobby joined the Marines. Paul collapsed and still struggles after his sister died. But I have my own problems and my wife is not going to stand for any more of this. We've seriously talked about divorce more than once, which is why she's at her mother's now. This has to work. I can't lose my family. If she comes home and I have no good news, she's packing up and leaving with the kids. The house will be gone. Damn it!

I don't know what Johnny Watson is going to do if I can't pay him back. She doesn't know about that because to make matters worse I borrowed from him of all people. He's just a guy at the mill but he's more than that. He and Buster Moze have a nice little racket going. Oh if she finds out about that (which she will if I don't get a job) I'll have no place to run.

It's not my fault! Thirty seven years old, two kids and heaps of bills to pay, I'm a loser. What time is it? 4:17? What's the weather? No not sunny – sunny – sunny. Ok stand up and pace, run this out of your head. Let's just go round and round the dining room table as fast as I can. Let's do it thirty seven times, the same age I am. One, two, three, four. I'm getting dizzy, got to keep going, go ahead and pass out if you like, I don't care anymore. Sixteen, seventeen, eighteen. Gasping for breath now – getting real dizzy – ow! How am I going to explain this goose egg on my forehead? Oh shit!

SIT DOWN! The dark seems to be gathering now. I can't see. Stare at the bookcase. Keep staring. Those are eyes from the top shelf blaming me, gnashing at me with those teeth. No they're books not teeth. I'm sorry. It's not my fault. "Then whose fault is it," she screams. And she screams and she screams and... What's happening? What's happening to me? Oh, I can't do this anymore.

Whisper through my hands again. I can't. I can't move my arms. Jaw is ridged like lock jaw. All of a sudden I can't move anything – except my eyes. I can talk to myself in my head and move my eyes. If the answer's no I can't live with the shame. Is this what it's like to be catatonic? Those WW I shell shocked guys couldn't move. What are you so scared of? "EVERYTHING!"

Move your eyes to the clock. 4:29. Move your hands to the brocade of the sofa. Rub – rub, stroke. Now your toes and feet. Stand and look out of the window. My chin is still clamped to my chest. Breathe and relax your neck muscles. Straighten up and breathe. It's time. Good or bad I've got to call. Breathe, phone number right here next to the phone. Glad the phone's not turned off yet. No, you dialed the wrong number, stupid. Do it again! Damn it! Ok it's ringing.

"Hello, Mr. Pittman's office."
"Hello, this is Tony Martino. I was told to call now to talk to Mr. Pittman."
"Ok, just a moment. Wait I don't know if he's still here. Hang on, let me check."
Oh my, I'm on hold. She doesn't know if he's still there? I need to know now. He said to call now. Breathe damn it! Wait, wait, wait.

"Hello, Mr. Martino? I'm still checking. He may be in the plant. Can you wait a bit more?"

"Yes I'll wait."

The clock says 4:36 already. I thought quitting time was 5:00. Watching the hands of the clock pass by me. Now 4:37. Raining sheets and sheets still. Dark, what's the weather report? Don't dare turn the TV on.

"Hello, Mr. Martino? Hold for Mr. Pittman."

"Hello, Tony? Oh that's right I told you to call."

(He hasn't even thought about it. He doesn't even have an answer. It's probably no)

"Ok, Tony, let's do this. You can report Monday and we'll get you started. You need to talk to Nesbit first. Come in about 9:00. We need a good man and there are a lot of them around. You'll have to prove yourself."

"No problem, Mr. Pittman. I can do the job. You'll see."

"Ok, well I'll see you Monday."

"Thank you so much for this chance."

"Ok, bye."

"Good bye."

Run to the bathroom. Good news so why am I throwing up now? Ok stop this. There's the door. Clean yourself up.

"Hi, kids. Hi Hon. Good news."

# THE CABIN

Gray boards stood watch -- sentinels scarred from years of wear and abuse. The marks on the weathered boards that once revealed the pink of youthful lumber, now sneered with the sadness of a neglected and resentful old woman. Some boards were missing and the grin of the dirty porch had lost a few teeth, but the roof provided shelter to hold memories. A trip to the cabin always entertained them with a surprise – when they were sure they'd lost their way, she would leap from the forest, arms wide and beckoning. She had been used. Once an eager, innocent and willing girl, letting them do whatever their perverted minds would ask, she now slumped old and forgotten. Tommy Ballenger felt a stab of guilt, visiting after these many years.

Tommy Ballenger was bringing his bride of less than a year, Stephanie Ballenger, née Johnston, to the cabin for the first time. Stephanie was born in Nova Scotia and emigrated to Brunswick, Maine where she attended high school. They met at the University of Maine. Though small, Brunswick was a real city with traffic and shops, stop lights and noise. She had asked Tommy about life in this small town, *Penobscot Mills*. They would be making their life together in this quiet Maine village. One stop on the tour had to be the cabin.

The first time Tommy came upon her was with Tony Martino, tromping in the woods, trying to get lost. Growing up in a small town in the midst of a forest, a form of dead reckoning developed. To actually feel lost and then use their skills to find their way back was a thrill. There was no beaten path – well north of town they crawled and squeezed through thick underbrush where the sun barely shone. Then, as if she were made of the forest itself, hidden in plain sight, she loomed in their faces.

She was never pretty. She had a small porch held up by two beams that were little more than trunks from trees the forest no longer wanted. Two windows faced the porch – without the glass she could no longer see, but still felt joys and sorrows from deep inside. She had one room and no other windows providing both privacy and secrecy for early sexual exploration or drinking or both. Her sightless eyes stared at Tommy and Stephanie as they approached with what amounted to reverence and slight trepidation. The maw of her doorway gaped – permanently yawning, unable to resist swallowing trespassers who poured down her throat.

"Wow, how did you find this place?" asked Stephanie, delighted with her Tommy for sharing his boyhood secret place she had heard of.

"Tony and I were trying to get lost and we nearly ran right into it," said Tommy flatly. His mind was on the things he knew had happened here.

"*Trying* to get lost?" Stephanie asked incredulously. "Who would ever try to get lost on purpose?"

"To know where you are at all times is the curse of living in such a small town and even in the woods I can point out, with reasonable accuracy the direction of town. It was a thrill to get lost and use the shadows of the sun, moss on the tree trunks, and the slope of the earth to get us home."

His voice trailed off as they stepped onto the porch, testing the honesty of each board. He was thinking about the first time he and Tony Martino found this cabin. No one knew who built it or to whom it belonged. They found three spent .410 shotgun shells and little else in side her. Imagination and fantasy began to work immediately. 'Cowboys and Indians' was a favorite game of theirs and it was easy to imagine having to hole up in this cabin and shoot through the windows (which still contained glass at the time). Shooting through the door, Indians were dropping all around them. They were truly naïve and never made the connection that, their friend, Bobby Rosebush, was almost a full blooded Penobscot Indian. No, to them Indians were out west and rode horses without a saddle. They would have to remember to bring their six guns the next time they came – if they could find the cabin again.

Tommy and Stephanie sat on the edge of the porch and dangled their legs over the side. Stephanie had firm legs from years of swimming. She had majored in physical education and would teach at the small school in the fall. A waft from the cabin brought Tommy's mind to the time Bobby Rosebush brought a pack of cigarettes to the cabin. Tony, Bobby and Tommy dangled skinny legs over the side. Tommy Ballenger did not want to try a cigarette. He was not then nor is he now a risk taker. He would be best suited to work at the bank and with his degree in business and finance from the University of Maine; he would rise quickly to vice president. But Bobby was coercive and peer pressure being what it was at nine or ten years old, Tommy did smoke a cigarette. Tommy wondered why he had lied to Stephanie about that. What difference could it make now – but the lie slipped easily out of his mouth before he could stop it. It wasn't good to lie to your young bride so early in the marriage. One should save it for later when bigger lies needed to be told.

Penobscot Mills was born around 1899 when the first construction of the mill was begun. There was no town at the time – people just came for the work. At a stretch of the Upper Penobscot River the channel straightened out and provided a perfect place for the mill. There were other paper mills on the river, but this was the one farthest up river. Upper

Penobscot Mill was the original but informal name. The Upper was dropped quickly – being too cumbersome, and became Penobscot Mill. The State of Maine map makers inadvertently added the 's' and the name Penobscot Mills was born.

Stephanie stood and crept toward the door opening – no actual door existed and Tommy knew why. Was she angry about the door? Did she hold a grudge? It was a fifth of Canadian Club and Bobby, Tony, Tommy, and Paul consumed the dregs. Paul stole the bottle from the roadhouse that was down the dirt road where he lived. "It was easy," Paul said. At 6:30 in the morning even the proprietor, Tim Nightingale, was passed out. Paul just walked in and took it from under the bar. Toward the end of the bottle, the spinning was inevitable. Lying on their backs was to court the need to throw up so Paul decided to swing on the door. Flung by Bobby, possessing a strong athletic frame which would serve him well in sports and eventually the United States Marines, he slammed Paul back and forth from wall to jam until a rending sound of torn ligaments vaulted the door into the corner of the cabin. She didn't cry then, Tommy remembered but she did later. Bobby's matches, discarded newspaper, and twigs and kindling provided the tinder. Boy Scouts were well taught but shouldn't use their lore to disadvantage. The fire blazing in front of her, she watched in horror as the boys danced around her mouth, and then she wept.

At fourteen Tommy brought Susan Beaumont to the cabin. She wore glasses that were rimmed in light blue and the oval lenses enhanced her almond shaped grey eyes. She had light brown hair pulled back in a ponytail. Most important to Tommy was that she had breasts. They weren't large yet but Tommy let his imagination guide his young eyes along a glimpse of white bra that ran to a soft, pale, barely exposed dint in the middle of her chest.

It's hard to say they were going steady because there was no "going anywhere" in Penobscot Mills, but they spent time together outside Bartlett's Drug Store. Susan Beaumont didn't consider herself pretty and fourteen is an awkward stage of life, still she made the effort. Tommy noticed the scent of powder, the slight shaping of eyebrows, and of course the white bra barely visible under a blue and white striped gabardine blouse. No one had touched Susan's breasts yet and Tommy had never touched one. In a bold move most unlike Tommy, when they were alone behind Bartlett's he asked, "Has anyone ever touched your breast?" Somehow Susan did not appear shocked but pondered the question for longer than Tommy could stand. Finally she simply said, "No, no one has."

In fact Susan had thought about the possibility that one day she would let someone touch her. Tommy was speechless. He'd ventured quite outside his comfort zone, so he said nothing and stared at Susan and her new breasts. Finally Tommy blurted, "There's a cabin in the woods that Tony and I found. No one goes there. It's pretty hard to find." Susan said, "I'd like to see it."

Mid-morning the next day, Tommy called at Susan's house near the north end of town by the high school. He led her past the clear cold spring into the woods, up and down the close terrain, until the brush was clawing them to turn back – but neither Tommy nor Susan listened. Finding the cabin, Tommy had no plan but strode into the dark without a word. Susan Beaumont followed, excited because she knew what she intended. Tommy simply put his hands in his pockets and stared out the window. He had no idea how to proceed. Fortunately Susan did. Grasping Tommy's right hand with her left, she watched herself guide him to her left breast, then she looked up at his face.

If Susan Beaumont had been a girl scout she would have recognized the pale, pasty look of shock on his face. He leaned and they began to kiss. Tommy had kissed before and so had Susan but both of their mouths tasted clean and sweet. Bathroom preparation just before the hike ensured a minty freshness. Her breast was soft and squishy and Tommy was careful not to squeeze too hard. Reaching inside her blouse he cupped his hand in her bra and they kissed some more. By now both teens were dizzy but Tommy wanted to see what this marvel looked like. Susan being the female in this duo and possessing more maturity took the next lustful if not logical step. Susan Beaumont reached behind her and unsnapped her bra. Tommy unbuttoned her blouse.

Susan's stark white bra slipped slightly to reveal a clear white breast. Tommy leaned down and the areola was exposed. Pink with a faint hint of soft brown and a tiny nipple, Susan stood looking at Tommy with exposed grey eyes. A couple of licks and a few swirls and it was over. Tommy Ballenger was surprised that it tasted like...skin – nothing special, just skin slightly sweaty from its hike in an innocent and soft white hammock. Tommy Ballenger and Susan Beaumont repeated this activity several times in the next few years.

She was warmly glad for them, this cabin in the wood. Having them inside her brought a smile and kept her roof peaked sharp. She was vexed, however, when Bobby Rosebush brought girls to her. His methods were not in keeping with innocent love. She would remember Tommy and Susan as a way to distance herself from other, harsh and disturbing occurrences she was forced to endure.

Jackknives – two blades maybe three, some with spoon and fork set for every formal occasion, useful for whittling and playing mumbley peg. Hunting knives – vicious sharp, pointed slicers of flesh for gutting deer and blood oaths. Every boy had one except for David White. David had no dad and his mom had almost no job so he stole a butter knife from the road house. Using a whet stone, he scraped and stroked and honed it as sharp as he could. David was always a poet and really didn't pal around like the other guys: Tommy, Tony, Bobby and Paul – roughing it up and falling from trees. Still his butter knife was pretty damn sharp.

The history of mumbley peg is as old as jackknives themselves. Originally the object was to throw the knife so it stuck in the ground as close to one's foot as possible. The boy who gets closest to his own foot wins and the name mumbley peg comes from a stick driven into the ground by the winner. The loser has to pull out the stick with his teeth, no doubt mumbling something about the winner. The boys played various versions of the game through the years – flipping the knife off of their fingers, chins, noses – then throwing the knife as close the other boy's foot as possible. Sober this was dangerous, *Canadian Club* made this game so daring only a fool would play it. They were fools.

She hated knives. Scars, inside mostly, were carved and scratched until graffiti was not even an apt description. Names, words, and pictures adorned the walls of the cabin. Without a door, she could only endure the foolish and dangerous antics of the boys.

"Who is Susan," Stephanie suddenly asked, snapping her head toward Tommy, with a slight scowl suggesting disapproval. Stephanie used the words 'who is Susan,' not 'who was Susan' as if to imply that Susan was a current fling.

"She was a girl I knew in high school," replied Tommy employing as little emotion as possible.

"This says, 'Susan loves Tommy,' Stephanie intoned.

"Yeah I know, I carved that years ago," Tommy interrupted.

Stephanie quickly uttered, "It also says, 'Susan loves every BODY.'"

Tommy peered through the motes of dust and sure enough there it was, 'Susan loves every BODY.'

"It must have been carved later when I went to college," he quietly responded. This flood of realization swirled around his head with the motes of dust. He had no contact with Susan when he went to college and lost track of her and interest. Guessing what she had been doing and to whom produced a version of guilt. But why should he feel guilty? College was a different place and he was different and moved on with his life. But being a coward he knew he didn't end it well or at all. He just left and that was that.

David White left Penobscot Mills when he was twelve. He reluctantly made up the fifth in this clutch of boys: Tommy Ballenger, Tony Martino, Bobby Rosebush, and Paul McLean. David hung out, but on the periphery. When he visited the cabin it was usually alone – time to think and ponder where life was taking him. Money was scarce for him and his mother and David White became the waif who ate at someone else's house two or three times a week. Other mother's came to expect him to show up and made a little extra. His mother was not well thought of but they bore no malice toward him. David spent more time with Angela McLean, Paul's older sister than the others realized. David White at nine and ten years old and Angela McLean, then thirteen and fourteen hung around the sand quarry. It was easier for David to talk to Angela because she didn't understand, being retarded somehow, and therefore couldn't judge his musings.

It wasn't so easy to talk to Bobby Rosebush about life, feelings, sensitivities, and what it all meant. Bobby was pragmatic and often teased David for being a sissy. The friendship David White and Angela McLean developed allowed both of them to rest in a place of safety like the hay loft in the back of a barn – quiet and dark and hidden. Then at ten years old, David White lost his friend. He heard the news in front of Bartlett's Drug Store. Angela and a homeless hobo, everyone knew as Old Blisters, had beaten each other to death. David went behind the store by the greasy trash cans and the sour rancid smell of discarded ice cream cartons made him vomit.

Incredulous as it may seem, most of the town was willing to believe that two people could in fact bludgeon each other to death. So callous were the feelings for Angela (the retarded girl) and Old Blisters (the guy who live in the dump) that no further thought was given to their deaths. David spent lonely times at the sand quarry until two years later when David's mother found him.

"I just got off the phone with your Aunt Dot in Brunswick. You're going to stay with her. We're leaving tomorrow. I'll pack your things. Now go play with your friends one last time," David's mother rattled off giving him no opportunity to respond. He crawled through the brush and approached the cabin. Bobby and Tony were there playing mumblety peg as usual. David had his finely honed butter knife.

She liked David White because he never did her any harm. Not like the other boys, scratching obscenities, burning her and smashing her blind. When David approached she knew there was a difference. He was angry and depressed. Depression comes, she knew, from not being able to escape current reality and having no expectation of rescue. Resignation hung down his sides and swung back and forth like his skinny arms. Tony and Bobby noticed it too. This was quite a feat for Robert Oliver Rosebush, who was already a matter-of-fact direct thinking man at twelve. The Marines would definitely be the place for him.

"What's the matter?" barked Bobby Rosebush in his best drill sergeant manner.

David looked Bobby in the eyes without flinching and slowly intoned, "My mother is taking me to live with my aunt in Brunswick tomorrow." Tears came from the desolation and entrapment David felt and dripped down his cheeks onto her porch. If anyone could notice, a faint groan wafted from inside the cabin. Tony and Bobby stared speechless and wished to say something, but they had no ready words of comfort to offer. Then David White paced into the cabin and drew his butter knife. It gleamed in a ray of light from the doorway which kept the motes of dust captive, as trapped as David felt. Slicing across the inside of his left arm he felt a sting and blood dripped. It was not a deep wound and would heal on its own but Bobby rushed in and grabbed David.

"Hey buddy, what are you doing?" spoke Bobby grasping David's arm.

David flipped his butter knife, gleaming and sharp until he held the blade between the thumb and forefinger of his right hand. The quick act of anger surprised Bobby and Tony as David White threw the knife which stuck in the wall, about a foot above the floor. "How's that for mumbley peg?" he cried and stalked off toward town. Tony walked to the knife and knelt to retrieve it.

"Nobody's going to take that knife," shouted Sgt. Robert Oliver Rosebush. "It stays where it is." And there it remained.

She felt for David. He had treated her with gentleness and respect unlike some of the others who invaded her. The cabin knew he was sensitive and the slight pain in her wall only made the parting more poignant. She had known David and Angela together and when David told her about how Angela was killed, she wept. It would be different without David to visit but she remained powerless to change any events that might occur.

Stephanie removed her shoes and creaked bare feet across the rough wooden floor. Turning she murmured, "What else did you do here?"

Thomas J. Ballenger, ESQ. as his business card read was not prepared to answer that question. In fact his birth certificate stated his name as actually Tommy and no middle name. He was dressed in a white short sleeve dress shirt, light grey slacks and ox blood tassel mocs – not the appropriate dress for hiking. But Tommy always aspired to the nattiness of dress. He had gone to the bank that Saturday morning on a mild June day in Maine to turn down a loan. He had been at the bank less than a year and old man Pittman had reluctantly given him a job and a chance.

Bernie Pittman was the bank president and his brother, Joe Pittman was the superintendent of the Penobscot Paper Mill. Together they comfortably oversaw much of the dealings in Penobscot Mills. They were decent folk but Tommy was not comfortable at all when Bernie said he had to turn this young couple down for the loan on a small house, just outside of town. Still, Tommy knew, as he was excellent at math, that this couple would not meet the requirements for a loan and so drew a breath and said "sorry." A banker must be above reproach, he convinced himself – no scandals and no skeletons.

Most of the peccadilloes that occurred in the cabin were harmless but not all. Stephanie swept the clouds from his mind when she interrupted with, "What's this, blood?" There on the floor close to the back corner was a splotch of rust. The color had deepened through the years and was still quite visible. Tommy's breathing became shallow. He reminded himself that he had to make Bernie Pittman trust him and a banker must be above reproach – no scandals and no skeletons. A small town like *Penobscot Mills* cannot abide nor easily hide indiscretion.

Noticing his difficulty, Stephanie said, "What's the matter, Tommy? What happened here? Where did this blood come from?"

"Mumbley peg," he mumbled. She was not pleased with this lie – not Stephanie for she knew no better than to trust her Tommy – no the cabin was not pleased. She had witnessed the truth – the indiscretion, the skeleton.

Tommy's thoughts turned to a gray day in early November. The Halloween had been surprisingly mild for a Maine autumn. Tommy ventured alone to the cabin to ponder his future. He was sixteen years old and working part time at Bartlett's to earn money for college. It was nice to be alone sometimes and the late afternoon soon drifted to dusk. Shadows began to thrill him and he knew it was time to head home.

Then a different shadow, an unexpected shadow entered. A man dressed in cut-off shorts, bare feet and bare chest scratched and soiled loomed at the door. He took two awkward steps to squint inside the darkened cabin.

"Tommy, something's wrong," Stephanie insisted, "Tell me!"

Tommy looked up at Stephanie's face and needed desperately to trust someone finally after telling no one for seven years. "I killed a man here when I was sixteen," Tommy inhaled in a gasp so deep it ceased his breathing.

Another woman might have recoiled in horror or been deeply suspicious, but Stephanie would continue to employ naiveté throughout her life and display a trust that at times was not earned.

"Oh Tommy," she comforted "I can't believe it. How did it happen?"
He began to relate the story.

The man continued to enter the cabin. He walked as if he was drunk but it seemed more that he was crippled. Tommy said nothing and scooted back toward the wall further into the dark. The figure continued to advance. Tommy didn't dare say anything, he hoped he hadn't been seen or at best the man would go away. On the gritty wooden floor scented with Canadian Club, Tommy's back flat against the back wall he recoiled in suffocation at the horrid creature.

The man realized someone was there. A startled string of unrelated vowels spewed from his mouth – moaning from fear and confusion, himself. The creature possessed a great voice which reverberated in the small filthy space. But the man continued forward.

Now, only a couple of feet from him, Tommy choked on his own fear and moved ever so slightly to his right. His progress was impeded by a chrome handle; David White's butter knife. Being left handed and in a moment requiring only impulse, he drew the knife from the wall, stood, stabbed, and ran.

He ran almost the whole way home. There was a little blood on his hand and a little on his pant leg. Sunday dinner was ready when he got home and his mom asked what happened. He just said he cut himself on a branch – the first of the easy lies he would tell in his life. That was November 5th. School was difficult to handle the next week, but early Saturday morning when it was getting really cold, he went back to the cabin. When he got there it was empty.

"Well Tommy, maybe you didn't kill him after all." Stephanie supported and held him in strong determined arms.

Tommy Ballenger never saw the man again and no account was forthcoming in the newspaper which came out only once a week. But even this act could cast doubt in Bernie Pittman's eyes if he ever found out.

Maybe an animal hauled the man away. Maybe he left on his own and bled to death someplace else. It was Tommy's secret for seven years and now his wife, Stephanie knew. She didn't seem to grasp the importance of keeping quiet. To her it was easily explained and nothing to hide. As far as she was concerned, Tommy should just go to Chief Pister and tell him what happened. But Tommy made her promise, never to tell anyone. He knew the cabin would never tell. But she had. She retained in perfect Technicolor the evidence for seven years.

Tommy entered the bank on Monday and Bernie Pittman was waiting for him. "Come into my office," Bernie said. Tommy went white but Bernie simply wanted to know how the loan meeting with the couple went Saturday.

"Oh fine, Mr. Pittman, just fine."

On a day when Stephanie went to Brunswick to see her folks, Thomas J. Ballenger, ESQ. carried a canteen and soap to the cabin to scrub his life clean.

Rutherford Nesbit crossed the darkened street to his house holding his side with his right hand and a sharpened butter knife in his left. Penobscot Mills was not a particularly violent town but Rutherford had been stabbed.

He walked in an awkward manner due to a lack of coordination not his wound. He had no friends and didn't much like people. For years his habit was to seclude himself in the forest atop a tall tree to spend his free time. Trudging through the forest shirtless in cut off pants fraying along the bottoms and scratched from the branches of trees he had been riding, Rutherford had come upon an abandoned cabin. Dusk had quieted the woods and darkened the interior. Rutherford entered, unable to see clearly. He must have been a sight with his strewn hair and dirty bare feet. He took two or three stilted steps inside. His eyes began to accept the dark and there he saw a shape at the back of the cabin, sitting still enough to become part of the cabin herself. Startled, Rutherford let out a series of sounds in a booming voice. The sounds were all vowels for he was too startled to close his mouth to produce a consonant. The shadow stood, stabbed, and ran dropping the weapon as he fled.

Rutherford realized it had been a youth who stabbed him and sprinted out the door and through the woods. The butter knife fell and Rutherford picked it up. *'What an odd weapon,'* the thought. The handle had tarnished but the tip of the blade was bright and sharp – honed deliberately to provide the owner with protection. The wound was not deep and would heal in a short time. Rutherford entered his house, cleaned himself, dressed the cut, and placed the butter knife in a wooden box he kept on top of his antique walnut wardrobe.

# THE LIZARD

Autumn comes early in northern Maine. Dry leaves skitter across the grass. The oak still holds her leaves and whispers in the wind as night gathers to announce another Halloween. What is it about the rustle of dry leaves on a dark autumn night that hijacks the imagination? It's as if you can hear voices in the wind – not of the dead but the unknown who are born screaming.

A trio of thirteen year old boys made up of Bobby Rosebush, Tony Martino, and Tommy Ballenger walk to a large plate glass window with paint in hand. The window belongs to the only hardware store in Penobscot Mills. They will each try to win the prize of a new Schwinn bicycle by painting a spooky scene. Lighted only by street lamps the object is to complete the art by midnight. The dark walk home is as anticipated as the act of painting. Perhaps fifteen to twenty boys and girls stand in front of their windows and wait for nine o'clock to strike from the town hall. It has long grown dark. The date is Saturday, October 25, 1958.

Penobscot Mills knows how to celebrate Halloween with gatherings and activities for children and adults alike. A square dance performs an allemande left and a promenade at the town hall for the grown-ups, teens paint windows, and youngsters bob for apples and run around the blocked off streets. This is only the beginning and it occurs the weekend before Halloween. This year school will be called at noon on Thursday, October 30 in anticipation for 'beggars' night' when the young and near young are left to scour the town for candy and to breed mischief. There will be no school Friday. The entire town gathers for costume judging, fun and dinner on October 31 every year.

The clock strikes nine and paint begins to smear and dab at the edges of each window and each imagination. The spooky house is a frequent theme – permutations through the years have leeched from literature such as Poe and oozed more recently from the movie theater of a Vincent Price offering, *House of Wax* which was released in 1953 but took five years to reach Penobscot Mills.

Considering the number of gutted deer, hung head down and slit at the throat that rock in the autumn breeze in Penobscot Mills, it's surprising that the paintings aren't bloodier. White ghosts flying from windows or across the moon, witches on brooms, and grave yards demanding 'rest in peace,' flow from brushes onto plate glass.

It falls to the high school coach, 'The Lizard' to supervise this quasi-ghoulish activity. Henry Lizotte is well liked. Thin, wiry with an oversized rib cage and skinny arms he was best suited to play basketball at which he excelled and his trophy case proves it. At six feet, one and a half inches tall, they went to STATE all three years of his high school career and won in his senior year. He likes his nick name and often moves like a reptile through the halls of Penobscot Mills High School in a mocking manner, not quite intimidating but always enjoyed. Another reason he has the nick name 'Lizard' comes from his psoriasis which was evident in the gym showers as a boy and in his basketball uniform on the court. Scaly red patches of sloughing skin on his back and arms gave his opponents pause and they kept their distance. Flecks of skin were evident on the hard wood floor after 'The Lizard' had played a game.

'The Lizard' strolled down the walk glancing at each window until he stopped behind Bobby Rosebush. "What's that going to be, Rosebush?"

"Globe and anchor, coach. My old man was a Marine and I'm gonna be one too."

"I don't know if that's spooky enough, Rosebush," worried Lizotte, stroking his chin.

"The U.S. Marines can be the scariest guys on earth when they want to," said Bobby, pausing briefly to regard his work.

"Suppose you're right, Rosebush"

'The Lizard' had noticed Bobby Rosebush in gym class as an all-around athlete. Good coaches are always on the lookout for talent. Bobby is half Indian (his father full blooded Penobscot), perfectly proportioned and competitive. The shadow that appeared between Lizotte and Rosebush could have been a fine athlete as well. Johnny Watson is slightly taller than average, large shoulders and hands but with absolutely no discipline. At nineteen this is his second year as a senior.

"Coach, my names not on the list," barked Johnny Watson whose defining personality trait is belligerence. He was referring to the team list for basketball that year.

"Yeah I know; rotten grades, you cut practice and start a fight nearly every time. I can't win with you, so you're off," said 'The Lizard' turning just perceptively to stare down Watson. Lizotte was a winner and his teams all loved him for it and performed better than their talents would normally allow.

"You don't want to do this to me," shouted Watson.

"Maybe I don't but that's what I did and it stays," spoke Henry Lizotte in a measured and metered voice not taking his eyes off Johnny Watson.

The boys and girls stopped and drew ever so slightly closer in a small gesture of support for 'The Lizard.' Red in the face, Johnny Watson slapped both hands on the globe and anchor then on Bobby Rosebush's tee shirt, then on down the wall to

Bartlett's drug store. He threw one fierce glance then stomped off with Buster Moze and Ralphie Pister, the chief's son in tow.

"Sorry Rosebush," said Henry Lizotte, "he's a real hot head alright."

"It's OK coach – mental discipline, that's what my Dad says. You can't beat 'um if you're mad." Henry Lizotte was impressed. Future Marine Gunnery Sergeant, Robert Oliver Rosebush was planning to get even.

When the windows were complete around 10:30 (it never takes till midnight), the globe and anchor had been repaired. Tommy Ballenger painted a spooky house with the traditional ghosts flying from windows. He always played it safe and would become a vice president at the town bank – no risks allowed. Neither Bobby nor Tommy would win the bicycle. Tony Martino should have won for creativity alone. His painting was a full figure of a white ghost with arms out-stretched and a white robe ending in a point at its feet. Two oval eyes and an oval mouth gave it a lonely soulless feel. This ghost also had a scraggly moustache and goatee. He had painted a beatnik ghost and the inscription read: "Like, boo man." Tony Martino would be the carpenter in the group, always looking for a new way to do something.

The young painters began their walk home. Henry Lizotte stepped to his 1957 Chevy Bel-Air two door hard top. It was two toned – white over aqua. He acquired it at the dealership in Lincoln, and it was his pride and joy. Bobby Rosebush, Tony Martino, and Tommy Ballenger turned the same corner as Johnny Watson had just an hour before and headed up the hill toward the elementary school and the town park. A cold breeze followed and chilled three elongated shadows which bobbed down the center of the street.

"Where's Paul?" asked Bobby. Paul McLean made up the fourth of the group. A fifth, David White had to live in Brunswick with his aunt.

"Home!" Tony replied. "Ever since Angela (his older sister) was killed by that hobo, he's been careful about the night. And you know how superstitious Paul is about Halloween. He'll be around for 'Beggar's' night though."

Street lamps at each corner of the park cast a faint 'X' marking the spot at the center where the white wooden band stand waited and watched. The boys approached. The encounter with Johnny Watson had put all three boys on edge. In truth there was no telling what Johnny Watson would do at any given moment. He was truly a creature of appetite.

The three parted, heading for their homes. Tommy Ballenger quickened his pace and walked North up Beech Street for the block and a half march to his house – his peripheral vision on high alert. He didn't want to be caught alone by Watson, Moze, and Pister. Bobby Rosebush turned right on Park Street to walk the three blocks past Eastern Avenue then up Elm another two. Tony Martino would cross diagonally to Church Street then up Maple two blocks.

Tony entered the shadow of a great white oak at the corner of the park. The breeze had freshened and the tree creaked as it waved at the darkened sky. Leaving the comfort of lamp light, Tony trod cautiously – eyes scanning the dim horizon for shadows and movement. He heard the sound of corpuscles as they bumped along the arteries in his skull and realized to his surprise he was sweating. His forehead was truly wet. A whistle came from his left and he jerked his head and froze – the wind through the chain link fence around the tennis court provided the punctuation. A deep breath and he continued.

The intermittent squeak from a bevy of swings to his right did nothing to belay his fears. Tony Martino advanced with measured stride closer to the hulk of the band stand at the very center of the park.

His stride slowed by half as he saw a light brown form, heaving its life upon the ground, just to the right of the band stand. Standing, he peered into the murk of stingy light and feared that this chest of waning life was Bobby's – same color of his shirt when they parted minutes before – or had it been longer. But how could this have happened? Yet the chest heaved in and out in deep gulps of air.

Tony Martino was horrified but he had to see. Edging closer in costly steps he finally reached the object only to find it to be a brown paper bag, caught by a fallen branch and heaving with each waft from the night. "Ok, this is ridiculous," said Tony to himself and he stalked quickly off toward the silent white wooden band stand, refusing to be fooled again.

He neared the band stand which just this summer had held his father who played baritone for Sousa's *The Thunderer*. Lattice around the base housed playground equipment and stared at him in multifaceted bee eyes. Tony's thoughts recalled a summer's day, egg salad sandwiches, potato chips, and hip flasks of whisky as he listened to the band blare a not all together perfect rendition of *Stars and Stripes*. Glancing behind him at the lattice and striding around the left, Tony's face was struck by wet, sticky fur. He shrieked in horror as he realized it was a dead cat, hung by the tail and moist with blood. Tony sprinted for home.

*"It was a one eyed, one horned flying purple people eater, a one eyed, one horned flying purple people eater. Oo ee oo ah ah, ting tang wala wala bing bang, oo ee oo ah ah ting tang*

*wala wala bing bang."* Bobby Rosebush's voice slammed down the street as he fairly danced toward Eastern Ave., then Elm. 1958 was no more immune from "novelty" songs than any other year. . These were *One Eyed Purple People Eater* and *Witch Doctor* which had come out in June. No need to carry a tune. These songs were nearly a-tonal, but fun to sing. Bobby neared the eastern edge of town and reached Elm Street, oblivious to anything going on around him. The streets were vacant. A light mist had begun to fall which doused the fire of his song and Bobby Rosebush fell silent then gasped and crouched behind a rhododendron bush.

The wind can make you think you hear voices just as a babbling brook can speak to you on a summer's day. These voices approached and Bobby hid inside the bush which had thankfully grown quite large over the years. Three thin and wavering shadows accompanied foot falls on gravel. Heading South on Elm Street toward the mill, Johnny Watson, Buster Moze, and Ralphie Pister descended to the paper mill. The mill was running three shifts, so external lights were visible from most anywhere in town but none of the boys worked at the mill. Bobby was curious but not enough to follow so he walked home, past Henry Lizotte's house and his Chevy parked in the drive. Bobby Rosebush turned and peered down Elm Street toward the Penobscot Mill before entering his house.

The 'Lizard' held his thumb on the tack for longer than he needed – as if letting go would mean letting go. He quickly raised his head which had been bent slightly, turned and walked toward the gym. Henry Lizotte lived alone since his wife died of pneumonia two winters ago. Bobby Rosebush witnessed the scene, stepped up to the bulletin board to read a note on a 3 by 5 card. *"Anyone knowing the whereabouts of a light gray cat, see Henry Lizotte at the gym."* The first bell on Monday rang and Bobby found his English class.

"You know class," Bobby's English teacher related, "Halloween customs can be interesting. For example, the figure of a witch on a broom would have been a terrible sight 300 years ago. You see, agriculture was not what it is today and in order to grow crops for next year, the farmer gathered the stalks of various grains they had grown and tied them together at the top. There would still be grain in the stalks even after the harvest. This was called the grain mother and would be undone in the spring and spread over the field to grow more grain. The fear was that a witch would steal this bundle of grain stalk, so the farmer put a stick in the top to disguise it as a broom; thus the image of a witch flying away on a broom."

*"Camouflage!"* thought Bobby, but he was thinking about "The Lizard's" cat. When class ended he found Tony, Tommy and Paul by the bulletin board. Tony's eyes were wide.

"I saw this cat Saturday night, tied to the band stand," spoke Tony with as little breath as he dared use.
"Let's tell 'The Lizard,'" said Bobby and the quartet walked directly to the gym.
"Was it dead?" asked Paul. "Did you see it? Was there blood?"
"Of course," said Tony.

Bobby pulled the heavy door to the gym and the boys stepped into an unlit room. 'The Lizard' had not turned on the lights. Then they noticed a sign cancelling gym class for the day.

The room was alive and each squeak, foot fall, and drawn breath echoed from bleacher to window to floor. The light in Lizotte's office was the only glow and they headed for it with respect for the cavernous space where 'The Lizard' had played and won years before.

Sitting at his desk, Henry Lizotte bowed his head – his great shoulders and long arms resting – stretching to each end. A white gym towel was spread out and he stared at an object in the center. The fur was no longer sticky, neither was it fluffy. Twine was still attached to its tail, the mouth – yawning was missing a tooth, and the sheen of jellied blood caught at the corners.

Tony spoke softly, "I saw her Saturday night on my way home but didn't know whose it was." Henry Lizotte raised a hand and all were silent. He gently wrapped the cat in a new white gym towel, cradled it, and walked out to his car.

Paul wouldn't move. The boys – now trio – began to walk back to class. Paul remained. No one in town knew that he had witnessed his sister's murder. Had seen her much the same as 'The Lizard's' cat. He had said nothing for years and now the sight of 'The Lizard' and the cat brought on a type of rigidity from which it was difficult to escape. Paul began to sob and walked in a stilted manner, out the front door of school and into the woods.

Monday after school, Bobby, who lived two doors from Henry Lizotte, helped him carve a shallow grave in earth which would soon be too frozen for use. 'The Lizard' shoveled the loam over his cat and looked at Bobby.

"Do you know who did this? Johnny Watson that's who, I can't prove it but I feel it as sure as I can feel my wife walking around this yard at night."

The town witnessed several dead pets over the years and talk of rituals in the woods at night kept most of the children at home. Bobby had suspected but no one would move to an accusation. Whatever evil happened in this small town, people simply resigned to fate. But future Gunnery Sergeant Robert Oliver Rosebush wanted to make his own fate.

Johnny Watson thought to himself, "The cat wasn't enough." The truth was that no one knew who killed the cat or any of the other pets – no one actually saw Johnny Watson during his ritualistic bludgeoning he had practiced deep in the forest for years; only Buster Moze and Ralphie Pister knew and dared not tell.

Tuesday after school, the four boys sat in a clearing just northeast of town, far enough from civilization to feel secluded. They discussed their costumes. The Halloween costume you choose says a lot about your self image; particularly in a small town like Penobscot Mills where people walk around town, naked in the way that everyone knows everybody's business. Who you are; who you hope to be; and the person in side that you want to hide provides the canvass for a complex painting of small town life. Halloween lets everyone pretend.

Bobby Rosebush always dressed in military garb and this year was no different – his father's shirt, too large with rolled up sleeves, green pants and boots with a Lone Ranger mask painted in camouflage, and helmet constituted his costume. Tommy Ballenger would wear a black costume of white bones and a skeleton mask. Tony Martino, who had been helping old Bill Mackenzie, a carpenter, would wear white painter's overalls, a hammer in the loop, and mask and painter's hat. Paul would go as a hobo. Dressing as a hobo was quite easy but Paul had another reason this year.

Paul's memories were rising to the surface like dead fish in a pond. The sight of Henry Lizotte's dead cat shocked him and his murky witness returned. That morning when Angela, his sister was killed, Paul knew it was not the hobo, everyone call 'Old Blisters,' who had killed her; though he couldn't see who it was. 'Old Blisters' had befriended and protected him and his sister that summer. Out of memory and perhaps respect for the old man, Paul would play the hobo.

A rifle shot roused the boys' attention. A second, then a third shot retorted through the forest. Someone was apparently taking target practice. Bobby led the boys toward the sound and crept ever closer to another clearing. There stood Buster Mose with a .22 long rifle in his hands. Poised and steady, standing 100 feet away he aimed at a square, silver can. *Plunk!* The shot pierced the can about three inches from the base and exited the other side. Standing to the side was Johnny Watson.

The quartet crept away. Tony was first to speak.
"That's a can of paint thinner. I've seen one at Bill Mackenzie's house."

A whispered comment Wednesday morning, outside the library provided Tommy Ballenger with insight as to the purpose of the can. Late on 'Beggers's' Ralphie was to place the can of paint thinner on Henry Lizotte's car roof and remove the cap to allow air flow. Moze was to shoot the can spilling paint thinner over the Chevy thus ruining the finish. Watson was to make sure no one removed the can before Moze shot it.

Lunch time at school, the four boys could hardly contain themselves. Everyone went home for lunch and had their big meal then. The boys ate quickly feigning school obligations and scouted Chief Pister's house. The can was visible from the vacant lot behind the Chief's garage. If the boys could switch the can with one of water Watson's plan would fail. Chief always kept a spot light on all night. There was no way to safely switch the can without being seen.

Tony Martino borrowed block and tackle from Bill Mackenzie and the four boys stalked toward Chief Harold

Pister's back yard at 11:00 Wednesday night This contraption contained two pulleys in the upper block and two in the lower with four strands of line running between them. Three boys could lower Bobby into the Chief's yard and hoist him back up. Climbing up and down a rope with a can of water or paint thinner would have proven difficult.

There was no concern from a crunch of leaves because the only tree was a mature white pine. The needles were spongy and made no sound. The future Marine, wooden block and tackle over his shoulder, climbed the tree, and attached the pulley on a great limb directly over the garage. He carried an additional line. When he was in place, Tony attached the silver can of water and swung it to Bobby who pulled it to his position. With his foot in a loop below the lower pulley and a hand on the can, the three boys lowered Bobby Rosebush into the Police Chief's back yard behind his garage. Bobby switched the cans and signaled for the boys to haul him up.

Climbing a pine tree is easy except for the sap and a good supply had become coated along the rope. As the boys worked the block and tackle, pitch began to build up in the block. Eventually the pulley jammed and would lift no further. Bobby lost is hold on the rope and his foot became tangled in the loop. Holding the can and swinging over the garage, Bobby was stopped.

Bobby found himself dangling head first about 10 feet from the limb of the huge white pine clutching a silver can. The block and tackle that Tony had rigged to lower Bobby into Chief Pister's back yard and behind his garage had jammed. Cursing, Bobby knew he should have just climbed down a rope and back up again. But Tony was so insistent that this would be better – eager to use what he'd learned from Bill Mackenzie. Tony, Tommy and Paul tugged on the line to free Bobby.

None of this was silent but most of the activity was quiet enough until the hitch in the plan occurred. Chief Harold Pister swung open his back door and peered into the lighted yard. Bobby Rosebush dangled head down and clasped a silver can of paint thinner as Chief Pister surveyed the scene. After but a few seconds the Chief went back inside.

Bobby reached for the ropes from the pulley and hoisted himself the ten feet to the limb. He decided not to climb down with the can for fear he'd raise the Chief again, the thin tin made a sound akin to thunder. He tied it to the limb with the extra line, untied the block and tackle and descended to the three waiting boys.

At a little after 10:00 in the morning of Friday, October 31 the day after 'beggar's' night, Henry Lizotte was in the basement of the town hall helping with the preparations for dinner that afternoon. Since his wife had died he took over the cooking and had brought a casserole for the pot luck dinner. He was stapling paper sheets to the tables when Johnny Watson strolled in.

"Hey coach, what happened to your car?" Watson said, hiding a mouth that turned up a little in the corners.

"What do you mean? What happened to my car? Did you guys do something?" and 'The Lizard' rushed out the door.

He reached his Chevy to find it in good shape as he had left it a few minutes before. Watson, Moze, and Pister approached slowly. No damage was done to the car and Lizotte stared at them.

"There was a silver can on top of my car this morning with a bullet hole through it but that's all," and Lizotte continued to stare.

Johnny Watson backed away and quickly paced up the hill toward the park. Ralphie Pister did not follow but instead walked away toward the railroad tracks. Johnny Watson seethed but there was no place for his anger to release.

'The Lizard' had heard a *'plunk'* late on 'beggar's' night and Bobby Rosebush heard it too. Lizotte didn't think anything about it but Bobby was waiting for it. Clear water flowed over Henry Lizotte's Chevy and Bobby smiled as he unwrapped a candy bar from his night of begging.

The boys kept their secret as a rite of passage. They had thwarted Johnny Watson. They kept quiet and only smiled as Chief Harold Pister related the story of the afternoon the next May when a silver can plummeted from the sky and slammed into his back yard as he was mowing the lawn. Other than the boys, only 'The Lizard' knew what had happened.

Henry Lizotte was sitting in the dark of his front porch that Wednesday night when Tony Martino arrived at Bobby Rosebush's house with the block and tackle. Paul McLean and Tommy Ballenger joined them and headed for the Chief's house. Lizotte followed. When Bobby became stuck, 'The Lizard' was ready to scale the white pine and rescue his student but he watched in awe as this future Marine escaped harm by his own skill.

'The Lizard' got a new cat. Watson, Moze, and Pister kept a low profile and Gunnery Sergeant Robert Oliver Rosebush had completed his first successful mission the night of October 29, 1958.

# THE LETTER FROM PENOBSCOT MILLS

When sensitivity collides with prejudice, a wound is created. Given enough of these wounds, the twig is twisted, the tree bent and life crooks skyward like a grand cicatrix etched in gray to whatever end has already been determine.

A yellow 1941 Ford Super Deluxe Coupe convertible in mint condition rolled to a stop in front of Bartlett's drug store on Main. A tall thin well-dressed man stepped out and cautiously sauntered to the curb where the trash can always stood. David White had not been back to Penobscot Mills in twenty two years since his mother abandoned him to live with his Aunt Dorothy Tebbits in Brunswick, Maine. The trash can was important, for that was where it began. One summer's day 'Old Blisters' (a hobo who lived at the dump) leaned against that very can with a toothless smile and eyes the color of green milk glass. David gave the can a tap with the toe of a well-polished leather shoe and heard the echo of two voices, searching for...something. The voices were two halves of one scrambled up brain and belonged to 'Old Blisters' and Angela McLean, a fourteen year old retarded girl.

David White had always been too sensitive – everything hurt. He not only sensed nuances, he saw them as clearly as if they were the specters of each person he knew, standing askew, haunting in pantomime what they were really thinking – what motivation was behind the spoken words. This left him shy and introspective. Angela was four years older than he when she died, but he loved her. He saw no nuances standing behind her, heard no wails of warning. He told her everything – she understood little and he loved her for it. 'Old Blisters' and Angela were savagely murdered twenty four years before.

Now perhaps his voice was added to the echo of that empty trash can. Looking west down Main, he gazed at the swags of red, white, and blue which announced the nearing of the town's 80th Anniversary Celebration of the founding of Penobscot Mills, Maine. He headed west toward the dump, past a new eatery, *The Tree Top Café* and the hardware store, gas station and barbershop. A letter from Paul McLean was stuffed into his hip pocket – a letter which contained a map of sorts; a map of Angela's murder. Paul was Angela's younger brother. The letter was a confession.

As he crossed Spencer's Brook he glimpsed the corrugated tin roof of 'Old Blister's' shack. Abandoned now for only a hobo would care to live there. David White imagined Paul, Angela and 'Old Blisters' munching on bologna sandwiches. Paul's confession was not of the murder itself but of his sin in not speaking up for his sister and the hobo. Paul entitled his confession, *A Murder of Crows* – a justified murder, for who would miss two outcasts in a town swaddled in prejudice.

Tony Martino hammered nails to wood slats and each rap retorted an echo making one carpenter sound like many. Tony the carpenter and old Bill Mackenzie were building the shells for float after float which would be pulled by pick-up, farm tractor, or auto in the 80th Anniversary Celebration. This summer, 1979, would be eventful.

They were five back then: David White, Tommy Ballenger, Bobby Rosebush, Paul McLean, and Tony Martino -- five boys who played, hunted, clowned, and risked together. Of the group, Tony was the person he wanted to see first. David White walked up Beech Street, drawn by the staccato of Tony's hammer. Would his boyhood friend recognize him? A tall shadow crossed his arm and Tony Martino paused and looked up. Neither said anything until a gradual tide of recognition flooded Tony's face.

"David?" Tony asked. "David White!"

He tossed his hammer from right to left hand and grabbed David at the elbow and forearm, shaking vigorously with a broadening smile. Tony was happy to see David. True friends, loyal friends, comfort friends were hard to achieve now. His wife almost left him when his business failed; he owed money to Johnny Watson, a childhood bully and now loan shark, and even his boyhood friend Tommy Ballenger the banker, had turned from him to secure his relationship with his boss Bernie Pittman. David, the sensitive one of the group would at least have sympathy if not understanding. Tony was glad to have extra work building these floats for the celebration. Maybe he could pay off Watson.

David White had liked Tony. They had played as kids and Tony didn't tease him like Bobby Rosebush.
"Did you come for the anniversary?" questioned Tony.
David felt the fold of Paul McLean's confession in his hip pocket, but he would wait to reveal his reason for arriving after these twenty two years.
"Sure, I thought my old classy Ford would look great in the parade," grinned David through grey eyes that revealed wear and sadness at the edges.
"A classy Ford, what kind?"

David reported the specs of the 1941 Ford and related how his mother had abandoned him to live with his Aunt Dorothy Tebbits. He told of how she took him in, befriended him, loved him, and eventually left him to live in Europe with a dashing, rich homosexual. Dot had given him the house and Ford when she left. David did not tell of the ghosts in the house that woke him at night and breathed in his face from time to time. Nor did David tell of the sight and smell of his Aunt's black and white photographic witness to a fruitless and lonely life, or of his own gallery of loneliness consisting of one photograph of a girl he loved in high school. He wondered where Stephanie was now.

Tony began to relate an account of the other friends who made up the group. Bobby Rosebush was a Gunnery Sergeant in the Marines, a career man who would be in town for the celebration; Tommy Ballenger was a vice president of the town bank, part of the inner circle which pretty much ran the town now; Tony Martino a carpenter with the mill, just hanging on financially; and Paul McLean a part time janitor at the elementary school (part time because of his drinking). Tony continued to tell of how Bernie Pittman, bank president, and his brother, Joe Pittman, superintendent of Penobscot Mill made most of the financial decisions in town – who can buy a house, which land gets to be developed, which stores can open and how much tax is to be paid. Penobscot Mills didn't have a mayor and apparently didn't need one. The final slap was that Johnny Watson, the town bully had become well off due to shady loans, "taxes" on businesses and homes, and a subtle leeching of marijuana onto the economic balance sheet of Penobscot Mills. How he got away with it, no one knew for sure but those who crossed Johnny Watson seemed to lose their household pets.

David remembered Johnny Watson as a bully from whom they all shied. David White decided to take a drive to where Angela's house used to stand. Paul said in his letter that she was buried by the river there.

"Whose car is this" crowed Johnny Watson as he kicked the tires of a yellow Ford convertible? He hopped in the front seat, pushed the starter button and threw her into reverse. Starting the car was easy but he needed a key to unlock the steering. All Johnny could do was back up and go forward. A small crowd chuckled.

As Johnny Watson was about to put her in reverse for a second time, David White said, "That's my car."

The chuckling eased but Watson's embarrassment was evident and a frustrated Johnny Watson was a dangerous Johnny Watson.

"Stupid car!" and he got out and slammed the door.

David White slipped behind the wheel, turned the key to unlock the steering and drove out of town heading for Angela's grave. He drove to the river where Paul and Angela's house once stood.

Paul McLean had said in his letter that the house was no longer standing and Angela's grave was unmarked but David needed to stand there and remember. The sunlight danced over rocks on its way down stream. The river was uncaring and unaware of the troubles of those in the town. It simply flowed, carrying nothing but itself and the sun. The significance of dancing sunlight was not lost on David White for he knew all too well of Angela's ability. It was her dancing which kept her at the roadhouse longer than she should and made men of dubious virtue, lust after her.

David looked down the dirt road, tree branches crowding overhead – he saw Angela dancing barefoot in the dust, smiling her dumb mindless smile, unaware of danger. He saw her being bludgeoned, felt her fall and imagined blood. Tears came and David recalled those days with Angela in the hay loft, heard the sound of her laughter, and he glimpsed again her breasts and hair between her legs. They had not been intimate for he was four years younger, but Angela had no sense of propriety. Her print dress hung to reveal her breasts and her knees spread to expose her developing womanhood. At ten, David was unmatched so he remained the voyeur. He could tell her anything – any dream, fear, hope. But she was innocent of danger as she walked that road for the last time. Flowers, well passed fresh were strewn over what appeared to be a grave – unmarked and untended. David was so snared in sorrow that he did not hear Johnny Watson approach.

"Hey pretty boy, what 'cha been dooin'? That's a fancy car you got. Don't like it when I been made a fool."

David said nothing and when he stood up he realized he was quite taller than Johnny. This gave Johnny pause and he stepped back a bit. Spying an envelope flopping from David's pocket, Johnny snatched it crying, "What's this? Is it the title to that car of yours?"

David White reached his hand, palm up, silently, desperately hoping for no confrontation. Johnny Watson began to open the letter when he heard a firm voice behind him. "Give-it-back."

Even in civilian clothes the carriage of a military man was evident – hair high and tight, solid chest, arms strong enough to handle any weapon, Gunnery Sergeant Robert Rosebush calmly stared. Johnny Watson tossed the letter at David and backed away, bowing in a mocking manner. "Yes sir mister Marine." He said and disappeared into the forest.

"Bobby?" David began, "but how did you…"
Bobby interrupted, "Tony told me where you might be. You know we all knew how you felt about Angela. You thought it

was your secret but we all knew, especially Paul. What actually is this paper anyway?"

"It's a letter that Paul sent to me in Brunswick. I didn't know why he sent it to me, but since you say everyone knew how I felt about Angela, I guess I know now." David fell silent and was obviously ruminating, deep in thought.

David was sensitive. Teasing, abandonment, and deep introspection had produced an intellectual, an academic, a writer who still shied from confrontation. His river led him to dead floating things in the nights of aloneness and to commune with ghosts – a man at the edge the living. Tony had felt the sting of prejudice being Italian and knew he had been run out of business by the Pittman's and left to beg for work at the mill. Behind the smile and firm handshake, hid some broken pieces of self – resigning him to his fate. Tony was proud of his work and his family was the most important part of his life. His river took him to the brink of madness when his wife left with the kids for a week. He was desperate. Paul was a drunk who had witnessed his sister's murder. Guilt had clouded his eyes and his reason. Tommy Ballenger the vice president had an easy way of slicing the truth into unrecognizable bits that could be easily swallowed until he knew neither truth nor lie and lived a life of delusion. Bobby seemed to be untouched by prejudice or slurs. He had been teased for being half Indian and his father had been maligned along with his mother.

The Marine stood calmly, looking at David until he was ready to reveal the real reason for returning to Penobscot Mills. David finally asked, "Is the cabin still there?"
"Yeah, I think so. It's been years since I've been there. Why?" Bobby asked.
"I thought we all might get together there and catch up."

"Sure, maybe. Where are you staying?" asked Bobby knowing there was only one motel in town.

"The Katahdin Motel," David replied. He needed the privacy because of his sensitivity and because he was not sure what he was prepared to do.

"Let's get the gang together tomorrow afternoon at the cabin." I'll talk to Tony and Paul, if I can find him, and you get Tommy to come. OK?" David asked.

"Sure, it would be fun. I'll bring a bottle," replied Bobby.

It was not much of a cabin. The boys found it when they were eight or nine, trying to get lost. It had one room, two windows (no glass), a doorway (no door), and a porch. Much had happened there – some good some not so. The cabin created a shared significance for the five youths now men. It drew them deep into the forest away from cares, away from town.

David was first to arrive. Pleased with himself for finding the cabin at all after twenty two years, he breathed in sweet forest scents mixed with what he was sure was stale Canadian Club. There had been some drinking in this cabin he knew, but this scent seemed too fresh to be the remnant of years ago. A rustle of leaves announced Tony's arrival.

"Wow! Surprised I could find the place after so long. I haven't had time or inclination to visit. There has not been much free time what with my wife and the two kids," Tony Martino rattled on.

"Who else is coming?"

"I found Paul and he said he'd come. Bobby is getting Tommy." David noticed a fleeting grimace on Tony's face as if he wasn't so keen on Tommy's attendance.

"I can't stay too long. I want to get back and bang out a few more floats before dark.

"Oh jeez Bobby you scared the heck out of me," Tony gasped holding his chest.

Appearing without sound, the Marine stood smiling with a bottle of whisky in his hand.

"You'd be surprised what I can do." The Marine was quietly composed, sure of himself and there was no boast in his manner, simply confidence.

"Did you find Tommy?" David wanted to know.

"Yeah he'll be here but his wife wanted to come along. No place for a woman but she thinks she knows you, Dave."

"What? How?"

"Don't know, just recognized the name I think, anyway I'm having a drink first," and Bobby Rosebush crack the seal and took a long pull on the bottle.

They heard the bickering before they saw the couple scrambling through the brush. The first face to emerge was Stephanie Ballenger née Johnston, Tommy's wife. David White froze.

"David, it **is** you. Remember me, Stephanie from Brunswick High?" With that she vaulted onto the rickety porch and threw her arms around David. He reciprocated out of simple reflex for he was stunned. Surely one of his Aunt's ghosts, who breathed mildew in his face those many nights alone, had become flesh. One of the many ghosts who helped him write his stories had followed him to Penobscot Mills. But it wasn't his Aunt's ghost. It was his own ghost from the black and white photo of

Stephanie Johnston that hung on his wall – the only girl he had loved – still loved.

"It's so great to see you again. How's your Aunt? Are your still living in the house. What are you doing now, and why are you here?" Stephanie exhaled the words has if she was running downhill, unable to stop until she reached the bottom.

"Yeah, I'm in the house and I graduated from Bowdoin in English and own half of the *Seven Seas.* Ronnie Polk runs the restaurant and I run the bar."

"Ok enough old home week," barked the Marine. "Have a drink little lady?"

Without a thought Stephanie grasped the neck of the bottle and took a swig.

"Now wait a minute," shouted Tommy Ballenger, banker. "You shouldn't be drinking in public, Steph."

"Oh shut up banker boy. We're not public; not here in the woods," the Marine interjected. Stephanie took another swallow grinning behind the bottle.

The bottle was passed but Tommy, dressed in white shirt, slacks and sweater tied around his neck as if he'd come from the tennis club, refused. There were no clubs of any kind in Penobscot Mills. No one had told Tommy.

The "catching up" ensued and as David quizzed Tommy about his job as a banker, Stephanie and Bobby were getting alone quite well discussing everything from war and physical fitness (she taught physical education) to the best whisky one could buy cheap; and this one wasn't so bad. Stephanie had begun to drink, not to excess or to interfere with her life, but as a way of distancing herself from life's disappointment – Tommy.

"So, Tommy."

"Thomas," Tommy corrected. I'm Thomas at the bank – more professional, more correct.

"Ok, Thomas what do you do?"

"I grant loans, handle foreclosures, and dabble in a little real estate for Bank Northeast. And you?"

"I own half a restaurant and run the bar; lounge really and I write."

"What…"

"Ghost stories"

Tony was uncharacteristically quiet especially when Tommy/Thomas talked about the bank.

"Yeah, Mr. Pittman and I have plans for Penobscot Mills. He calls it his master plan."

"Sure!" spoke Tony. It was clear that this utterance was not supposed to be heard.

"You know I did everything I could to help when your business failed," Tommy defended.

"Failed? Failed? I was closed down and run out and you know it. David, people have to get a loan to build a house or add on. And the only place to get a loan is *Bank Northeast.* And they won't lend you money unless you use Pitman Contracting and Lumber."

"Is this true Tommy?" Stephanie accused.

Tony fell silent, breathed a snort through his nose and looked out at the forest. It was clear he wasn't continuing this accusation.

David wandered into the dark safety of the cabin. Darkness was the most welcome environment for him. Years of seeing, breathing and smelling his Aunt Dot's ghosts in that house on Belmont Street had provided him with stories to write and perverse comfort.

The marine evaluated his squad and shook his head.

"Well, Tommy? Is it true?"

"No, of course not. We grant loans to plenty of people who don't use Pittman; it's just that most people prefer to deal with us."

'US' was too strong a term, even for Thomas J. Ballenger, Esq. as his business card read. True, he was privy to much of Bernie Pittman's deals, but he only wished he was in the close circle. Intrigue is an opiate for some and Tommy was addicted. He came home from the bank later and later. Stephanie, the ever naïve and trusting spouse simply pined and drank; not to excess, only on the summer school vacations and on weekends, but to enough to feel…less.

"We need to leave, Stephanie. You know the dinner we have tonight; I want to get ready."

"Gimmie the bottle, Sergeant!" and Stephanie took a long swig.

Rosebush was liking Stephanie more and more, though her gaze repeatedly turned toward the cabin's missing door and into the dark where David stood – silent, still and lost. None of the group could guess that David White was entertaining his Aunt's ghosts at that very moment. David could write ghost stories easily because he simply took dictation. The exhale of mildew through dirt filled mouths provided stories only they could tell.

"Not now!" David commanded, and this particular ghost named Maude rose through the ceiling and was gone.

"What do you mean not now? David, I said what's in this letter from Paul that Bobby's been talking about out here?" Stephanie asked.

"I want to wait until Paul arrives."

"I'm here." Paul McLean stepped on to the porch like a seagull back from his flight across the Atlantic; unsteady and dazed.

"I know why people use Bank Northeast. They're afraid of Watson -- of what Watson would do, could do, will do."

"I've never seen Watson at the bank," offered Tommy.

"Nobody asked banker boy, but what you're suggesting is that Watson and Pittman are tight."

"What's in the letter, David?" Stephanie was insistent and a little tight herself.

David looked at Paul.

Paul McLean began to softly recount the events of that summer twenty four years ago. He waxed poetic at times but pathos was the primary vehicle.

"I watched her walk down that dusty road to our house one last time after dancing at the roadhouse all night. I'd seen this many times and warned her, those men weren't her friends. But she couldn't see it or understand I guess. That was the summer we became friends with 'Old Blisters.' We hung out at his shack. It wasn't as bad as you might think. Angela seemed to get along better with him than I did. Maybe deep inside those two rattle heads there lived a common language. Anyway, he was always watching even when we didn't see him. Usually up in a tree.

"It all began when 'Old Blisters' leaned against that trash can outside of Bartlett's drug store. He had a whole sack full of five cent bottles. Bartlett wouldn't let him in so Angela dragged the sack in for him and bumped into Mr. Watson, Johnny's father. He was grabbing at her and her dress came up over her head. She had panties on this time thank goodness. 'Blisters' stared at him and Mr. Watson let go. We ran to the dump and so began a few weeks of bliss.

"I can see now as clearly as years ago silhouettes against a bare and cloudy sky moving toward her – four of them, three smaller and one fatter. Angela got her dress almost completely torn off. That was when 'Old Blisters' jumped from the tree and the four ran away.

"I stood at the screen door in relief for maybe two minutes – not long. Then I swear it was Johnny Watson who crept up with a log and with one blow to the side of 'Blisters' head, down he went. Then he slammed the log into Angela five times; counting each blow as if he was killing a snake, 'one, two, three, four, five,' then he ran.

"Have you ever seen Johnny Watson beat a cat to death? I have. It was the same way Angela was murdered."

Paul stopped. All were silent.

Stephanie leaned toward Bobby and whispered, "Gimmie the bottle, Sergeant." Stephanie softly breathed and took a slow sip, eyes filling.

Sitting on the edge of the porch, bare legs dangling, shoeless, she began to think: *a girl gets murdered, and a man also and no one investigates? Two people cannot beat each other to death. It's impossible. A guy kills cats for a living and everyone is scared of him, yet he walks free with money in his pocket. I have a husband who knows more than he's telling and comes home later and later. This is not what I had imagined when I got married.*

Paul McLean had begun this with his letter to David White. David, never forgetting his affection for Angela, had continued the dialog and brought the boys together. When he arrived in town he was not sure what he was prepared to do. Everyone, including Stephanie, was about to find out. One of his Aunt's ghosts, Maude had told him what to do.

The ghosts have no sense of self but see the world as in a dream where anything is possible and nothing is risked. The stories they told were fantastic because space, time, the firmness of the earth itself did not exist for them. It could be said that David was imagining his ghosts – David thought it might be true but he didn't care. They were comfort companions who helped him write. When they appeared the scent of mildew from that dark corner of the wet basement behind a huge heaving, raspy furnace where shadows thrilled, would fill the room almost to suffocation. Opening their mouths, loose earth tumbled out as did the words.

Maude had told David to confront Johnny Watson as if he were a pal who had always been in awe and get Watson to brag about the murder as he most surely wanted to do.

"WHAT!" shouted Tommy Ballenger. "Are you kidding? Confront Watson to get him to brag about killing Angela? You're nuts. Come on Steph." He grabbed her by the arm and led her through the woods. Stephanie Ballenger née Johnston pulled free and stomped back to the cabin. Tommy stopped and stared into the woods.

"Ok so who's going to do it?" demanded Stephanie in a tone that dared the group to volunteer at the same time hinted of an unspoken promise – a promise of admiration, of adulation, or maybe affection.

Each endured their own rivers of fate and had their own reasons not to confront Johnny Watson.

Stephanie fanned her gaze from one candidate to another.

After an excruciating ninety seconds, Paul spoke. "I can't do it. I don't have the nerve and she was my sister. Johnny would never brag to me."

"I'd like nothing better than to beat a couple of fists into Watson's face, but I'm not gonna buddy up to him," Grunted the Marine.

"I'll do it," volunteered Tony.

"I'll come with you. Maybe we can make him mad enough to spill," offered David White, the writer – afraid of confrontation. Maybe with Tony for support he could pull it off. They would meet tomorrow after church.

Tony Martino floated face down in the company of a thousand pulp logs that accepted him as their brother and promised to travel down the river with him to the end.

Hammering at the door of the Katadin Motel woke David White.

"Get dressed Dave," barked the Sergeant, "You've got three minutes."

Disoriented, David pulled at pants and shirt, ran his hand through his hair jumped into shoes and staggered out the door.

"What?"

"Tony's body was found early this morning in the Penobscot River with his face beat in."

"Who?"

"I'll take you. I'll drive."

Chief Ralphie Pister was on the scene and pronounced his findings.

"Fell into the pulp raft drunk and got slammed by the logs," Chief Pister reported to no one in particular.

David White had eaten dinner at Tony's house with his family that night and Tony drove to the motel with him. He walked to home so he could think along the way. His wife was frantic.

The grassy river bank was slippery and Tony's wife careened like a log through a sluice into her husband's arms.

"He never came home last night. I called everyone – even you Ralphie and no one had seen him. He never stayed out late. He always tucked the kids…" She surrendered to a mumble of grief and sobs.

By then Paul and Tommy had arrived. David looked at Bobby who snapped an eye at Tommy, who bowed his head and glanced at Paul.

"Hey, Ralphie" called the Gunnery Sergeant.
"Chief Pister to you Rosebush!"
"Where was Johnny Watson last night?"

An uncomfortable pause was finally followed by:
"We played cards alllllllll night. And as Chief of Police and Coroner, that's all there is to say."

Tony Martino had walked home that night alone and was confronted by Watson.

"I bought your home loan from Ballenger, so now I hold the note on your house and I want my money now," spoke Johnny Watson firing and spitting his words like bullets to Tony's chest.

It was as if he were being assaulted, for his family, his wife, his home were becoming forfeit. His river left only one choice. He raised his arm to strike. Johnny Watson slapped him beside the head. It was a ball of lead attached to a spring and a small handle – a blackjack. Tony went down immediately, was beaten in the face and dragged to the river.

No official investigation was conducted and the citizens of Penobscot Mills believed as anyone would that Tony Martino had ended his life in final desperation. Tony had been stressed and beleaguered for many months. It was just a matter of time.

Tommy Ballenger finished his dinner party that Saturday night and tucked his tipsy but delightful wife into bed then took a walk. Watson appeared and startled Tommy.
"What's been goin' on?" demanded Watson.

Tommy related the conversation at the cabin and the attempt to implicate Watson in Angela's murder. Watson proceeded to arrange for the purchase of Tony Martino's mortgage on his house.

"Yes Sir Mr. Watson. It will be done," said the eager and naïve Tommy.

Johnny whistled on his way to Chief Pister's house.

A third citizen of Penobscot Mills was laid to rest without a sound.

# THE TREE TOP CAFÉ

Audrey Marie Nesbit slipped her shoes off and dropped them beneath the sign which read: "No shoes, no shirt, no service." She smiled at the irony but she was the owner of the café and barefoot was her preference. Gazing upward at the two story expanse – her café consisted of nine levels, landings, and lofts with fichus trees, ferns, and philodendron in abundance. She and her husband, Rutherford had launched their café in 1964, fifteen years before when they both quit their jobs – hers in a book store and his as paymaster of the Paper Mill in Penobscot Mills, Maine.

The Café closed Sunday and this afternoon was watering time. The plethora of plants required almost an hour to make the rounds and the nine levels with botanicals on each made it a task. Rutherford was in Bangor pricing a wrought iron spiral staircase. The plan was to connect the lofts, where most tables rested, to the staircase. Transportation and installation would be a problem.

Audrey gripped her toes on the hardwood floor – her calves flexing as she went to retrieve the long white hose that she used to water her plants. She finished the ground floor and stepped to her right to ascend to the next level. She crept up level by level pulling the long white hose as she went until she reached the ninth and highest level where two small round tables stood. Windows along the front facing Main Street ran up one floor only so the top loft was darkened especially if the lights were off.

Audrey Nesbit hung the hose on the railing and a specter of naughty expectancy waxed and waited with her. She unbuttoned her blouse, removed her skirt, slid her panties to her ankles and unhooked her bra. Standing naked in the dim light she dropped her clothes to the ground level and sat at a table in the corner. If her husband had not been in Bangor, that would have been his cue to ascend the levels and join her. Every Sunday afternoon they would meet in the locked darkened Café for a tree top tryst.

Sitting at the darkened table, Audrey gradually realized Rutherford was not there to retrieve her clothes and bring them to her. She would have to descend nine levels naked; but putting off the inevitable was one of Audrey's sumptuous skills, so she sat to ruminate, and remember. The dim light was a muted horn of soft jazz which Audrey allowed to enter her and gradually become her. Dishes sat quietly in the cupboard, conversations were stilled and the calm tugged Audrey Nesbit to review the past.

A glance down to the second level where wooden lattice rimmed the railing reminded her of a time when she was six. She found herself under the porch peering through wooden lattice, hiding, safe and alone. Company had come from down state – company she didn't know – an aunt and uncle, a girl cousin who was eight and an older boy who frightened her. She couldn't say why she was hiding, crouching, cringing behind a protective array of bee eyes, but her heart beat relentlessly. The boy was tall, skinny with too small of a nose for his face and long crooked fingers.

Audrey smiled to herself. Fantasy and imagination often led her to pretend. *This boy was a ghoul, an unnatural being from a frozen world where little girls were eaten.* Audrey Marie couldn't help herself then; she simply ran headlong into the first river which flowed past and let it sweep her away. Sometimes the river was benevolent and sometimes it was malevolent. At thirty-nine she managed her thoughts most of the time but for much of her life, especially as a child, she remained shy, bookish, and far too creative.

Third grade Audrey sat by the window in the back of the class, the lid of her wooden desk held up by one hand as she searched for a blue crayon. She lowered the lid and the hole which once held an ink well, winked. Audrey winked back and grinned. Surveying her classmates to see if anyone had seen this phenomenon, she was delighted that her ink well was playing with her. Recess was spent mostly alone, staring through a wire fence, dreaming about some movie star. The ink well winked again. This was impossible she knew but just as she was about to dismiss it, a third wink occurred. Had she not been sitting by the window her ink well would not have winked, for the sun through the branch of a white pine cast an intermittent shadow allowing her ink well play with her.

"Audrey Marie Cook," spoke her teacher. "I asked if you would mind coming to the blackboard to do our multiplication."

"Yes Ma'am," Audrey replied and dangerously approached the blackboard. Any public action was difficult for her – she was quite capable of performing multiplication but performing in front of the class was frightening. After completing the mathematics, she returned to her new friend the ink well but by then the sun had shifted and refused to wink. Audrey, undaunted, could see that the ink well was as exhausted as she was after performing for the class, but even though the sun through the white pine ceased to provide animation, Audrey winked and the ink well winked for the remainder of the afternoon.

After the last bell Audrey Cook walked across Beach Street to Penobscot Mills' only park. The park was marked with an "X" of paths from each of four corners. They met at the center where a white wooden bandstand slumped. The black, Mary Jane patent leather shoes her father insisted she wear snapped on the sidewalk but Audrey felt uncomfortable in them especially with the white ankle socks with lace frills. Her mother bought them for her just before she died almost a year ago Her father (the high school history teacher) still grieved, heaving deep sighs from his large chest; so sensitive Audrey obliged her father and wore the shoes even though they were now small and pinched her toes. She bent down, unbuckled her Mary Janes and stuffed her socks in each toe then proceeded barefoot.

Audrey ran ahead to over-take a younger girl who also walked barefoot. Angela McLean walked barefoot for a different reason than Audrey. No new shoes would be forthcoming from her father soon and Angela's mother died two years ago giving birth to her brother, Paul. The girls ascended the bandstand and walked to the very center where the parabola of a roof created an echo and each girl screamed with glee – flooding little girl squeals over the park – squeals that become the legacy even of grown women when they retain the girl inside and are unashamed. Each girl then walked to opposing edges of the bandstand and spoke softly. The parabola allowed Audrey and Angela to communicate in a secret way that no one else could hear. Angela waved goodbye and walked home while Audrey Marie Cook took Maple Street north.

Maybe it was the dim silence of the ninth level at the *Tree Top Café*, but thirty-nine year old Audrey ached for the eight year old girl as she entered the house, always silent, always alone after school. Her father would be grading papers for about an hour at the high school which provided Audrey unwelcomed alone time to miss her mother. It was a freak accident as her mother was walking along the sidewalk in front of Bartlett's Drug Store. An old man in a pick-up suffered a stroke, became unconscious and veered onto the sidewalk. Audrey's mother was thrown through the plate glass window and died as she hit the green and white terrazzo floor. It was painful for a seven year old but now at eight and after almost a year, Audrey had re-lived and remembered many afternoons until she came to feel only a slight catch in her throat.

After all, Audrey Marie possessed reliable methods of escape. Fitting one leg then the other through the spokes of her foot board on the bed, she grasped the curved maple rod and began steering her lobster boat back to harbor. Bare eight-year-old feet dangled over the side as salt spray cascaded down her face and hair. Gripping tightly and leaning back at arm's length, the skipper guided her craft up one great swell and down another. She liked the sea when it was active like this and never got seasick. Audrey leaned to starboard then to port, wrenching her ships helm as she did, willing to let it break before she did. Frenchman's Bay would provide good anchorage and calm waters if she could make it. Just then a crack echoed over the boat threatening to plunge her vessel to the bottom.

"Audrey Marie Cook! What did I tell you about treating your bed this way?" Audrey's father had arrived home and the crack had come when he opened the bedroom door.

"Sorry, Daddy."

Norman Cook looked at his daughter's legs thrust through the spokes of her bed and noticed red marks on her feet.

"Your shoes don't fit anymore do they." Her father said. "We'll get you something new to wear."

"Oh Daddy, Keds? Black high tops?"

Basketball shoes were not worn by little girls in 1948 but whatever social stigma Audrey might have incurred would not be noticed as she proudly returned to school next Monday wearing black high tops and a plaid jumper. Norman Cook was a good father, taking his daughter on many day trips and a summer vacation but raising a little girl, possessing no fashion sense, helped to encourage an independent and strangely clade tomboy.

Audrey's hair was drenched with salt spray and her bare legs dangled through sturdy bars of the railing on the ninth level of the *Tree Top Café*. She had not piloted her lobster boat for many years, but the 39-year-old remembered how. She gradually became aware that she was naked with her legs through the bars in full view of Main Street. She extracted her feet and sat in shadow again.

Audrey was not invisible in the physical sense but in a practical sense. By keeping an expressionless countenance and a still body she could be standing near a group and against a wall and not be noticed. It was when she was eleven or twelve that she began to employ this power. The new sight was like watching pollywogs in a jar – she could see everything they did but they were oblivious to her. She saw Brenda walk to a clutch of girls from their class and witnessed the girls turn just slightly to avoid eye contact and Brenda walked away. It is true she was quite poor and the white anklets she wore were gray but that kind of prejudice ran deep in this small town. Her print dress was well worn before it became a donation from a neighbor but Brenda would choose another route to notoriety.

Audrey also saw budding romances. The owner of *The Treetop Café* recalled standing in plain sight watching a boy and girl kissing. On a path just west of town ran a dirt road which led to the dump. Coming upon them, she stepped to the side of the road and sat on her haunches, arms resting on her knees while Brenda kissed Johnny right on the mouth for a long time. All three of them were twelve at the time. This was the moment which launched Audrey into a romantic river from which she never escaped.

Johnny Watson had blonde curly hair – always a little too long – and a short smile which projected mirth and danger simultaneously. He sat near the door since the principal frequently hauled him out of class for one infraction or another. Audrey sat in the back near the windows. She had always been attracted to him but since the kissing scene she fantasized continuously. Audrey could feel his lips and small mouth on hers and strong arms and shoulders around her.

This was not the limit to her fantasy. She walked with Johnny to school every day, holding his hand, rubbing her thigh against his – feeling the thrust of his tongue in her mouth, inhaling the sweat from him after basketball practice. Audrey had an acute imagination yet Johnny and Audrey never spoke; never had a relationship; never saw each other, but Audrey knew it all. It was about this time when she began climbing trees deep in the forest. Further and further she went and higher and higher she climbed. If she was too shy to engage in other people's lives and had to live a life alone then she might as well separate herself completely. She swayed upon tree tops for hours and fantasized and ached. Only Angela McLean kept her company; a retarded girl from the northeast side of town.

Angela was a girl of perfect bliss, perfect peace, and perfect innocence. She looked up to Audrey, two years older and followed her around in awe and joy. Audrey didn't mind. Both of them were invisible and Angela embraced every fantasy Audrey could devise. Angela knew she was not smart but didn't have a proper perspective. She read from different books and performed simple one digit to one digit addition – no subtraction yet. None of that mattered when the two 'A's were together. The two 'A's they called themselves as they slipped through town and nearby forest unnoticed.

People in town saw Angela as 'tetched.' She made baby talk when she was nervous as a way of producing laughter in others and defusing an awkward situation. But being limited is never complete. Angela knew they were laughing at her and why. She could not read well, or speak so well but she saw through artistic eyes. She danced -- danced to a rhythm unknown to anyone, not the beat of a different drummer but the throb of her mother the earth. This throb drew upon an ancient nature, one which was unfelt by others, especially her father. A brute of a man, he caused Angela's retardation early during a drunken beating.

She lived with her father and her younger brother, Paul. She slept in the one big room with Paul. A stove, refrigerator, a couch and one chair – no room for a kitchen set was heated with a cast iron stove. It was a cramped, lonely life with no privacy so days spent with Audrey atop a tree, deep in the forest were welcome.

One fantasy game they played often was 'enchanted forest.' Audrey created imaginary roles for them. She was Phoebe, princess of elves who was most beautiful and wise. Angela was Zephyr, queen of the breeze – a being who could slip through any space unseen.

Soft yellow grass cushioned their feet as Audrey led Angela to a glade she had found. Sunlight gleamed off black-eyed Susans and bounced through tall grasses leading to taller trees. Audrey, fifteen and Angela, thirteen were Phoebe and Zephyr stalking a great beast that lived at the edge of the glade. Its eyes glowed red frightening the town's people at night but Phoebe and Zephyr had to chase it away. Just then the girls saw two bare legs rising up from the grass in a **V**. Creeping backwards and up a tall maple, the pair ascended to a height where they could see. Johnny Watson and Brenda had their pants off and were thrusting against each other. Audrey looked at Angela and then back to the scene.

Audrey was both repulsed and attracted; each wrenching her first to starboard and then to port. The sex act was very disturbing and at the same time enticing because her Johnny was a participant. She actually felt betrayed even though no communication or contact had ever occurred between them. Unlike Audrey, Angela accepted the scene as part of life – as part of what she had witnessed in her house with her father and women. The girls left the 'beast' alone to ravage as he will and returned to town.

For days after, Audrey obsessed about Johnny. Each glimpse of his bicep or flex of his forearm sent ripples of desire through her. She could win Johnny back. She could defeat Brenda. The fact that there had never been a relationship did not deter fifteen-year-old Audrey. She became hungry and the river into which she had now flung herself was swift.

Thirty-nine year old Audrey shifted her bare bottom on the wooden chair at the ninth level and squirmed just a bit at the memory of her obsession and remembered when she had begun to climb trees deep in the wood and slowly remove her clothes. Riding the very top of a tree, unseen by anyone,

Audrey Marie Cook rocked herself into a sensual nest. A smile about her face, toes clutching a branch, she ran deeper into fantasy. She would have been mortified if anyone had seen her. This was simply her way of continuing the fantasy and allowing herself to feel a little naughty. She felt different, more courageous on top of a safe tree. Many years later she would meet her husband, Rutherford atop a tree such as this.

Each of the three outcast girls had found their personal method of coping. Brenda became notorious as Johnny Watson's 'girl.' The other girls in class did not approve, but they never approved of 'dirty' Brenda anyway. Audrey coped through fantasy which became portable, faithful, and safe. Angela chose an artistic river, one which would be fruitful and dangerous.

On her back with legs in the air, Brenda saw the two girls in the tree and she smiled. Even Brenda didn't know exactly why she smiled but the thought of someone seeing her with Johnny gave birth to a kind of pride. Love and acceptance are to be found in many ways and each of them is specific to each person. Brenda would eventually give birth to another kind of pride, a baby girl. Brenda quit school, went to work at the mill but never coupled with Johnny again. That was ok with Brenda. She experienced a love one only gets from a child. Brenda was a loving and good mother and provider. Her girl finished college and came home to live and work in Penobscot Mills.

Angela McLean leaned against the rough wooden side of the roadhouse, a half mile from her house and let the music in. Angela was fourteen that summer, dancing in the dust by herself – a dance that was inspired and possessed. Inhibition was not part of her being, she let all of the music and rhythm flow through her. It was like the rivers of fantasy that Audrey Marie Cook swam – swift, dangerous, and heady. Tim Nightingale, the bartender, noticed her as he poured the bin of empty liquor bottles into the trash.

"Hey, you dance real good," said Tim. "Why don't you come on in?" Stepping carefully, Angela slid her bare toes onto the dusty, wooden roadhouse floor. The jukebox was blaring *Rock Around the Clock* by Bill Haley. Angela stared for a minute but soon was swaying and stepping to the beat. Chuck Berry was up next with *Maybelline*. Other stars like Frank Sinatra, Doris Day, and Gale Storm flooded her ears and fed her dance until the crowd of sweaty men put their glasses down and watched. But when *I Hear You Knocking* by Smiley Lewis came on she had the entire floor clapping. Angela was in a state she had only dreamed of. Intoxication was the only word for it. In the summer of 1955 Angela became an unwitting siren to men of dubious virtue.

The fact that she was fourteen didn't matter. Boys of sixteen were there watching too. In this small town kids grew up quickly, often on their own. One of the teens was Johnny Watson.

This was also the summer when Angela and her younger brother, Paul began hanging around the dump. Old Blisters was a hobo who lived there and Angela got along well with him. He was probably schizophrenic and definitely out of touch with reality but he took good care of them. Hanging around at the dump was not a problem but dancing many nights until early hours was a problem.

The thirty-nine year old Audrey paused at the next part of the story. The Café was not silent any longer. Blood pumped through her ears as her heart beat faster. The men at the roadhouse were becoming more and more lustful until a group followed Angela home early one morning before sunrise. Audrey didn't know the whole story even now but there was a scuffle and Angela's dress was torn off. Apparently Old Blisters appeared and chased the group away. All anyone would say was that both Angela and Old Blisters were found bludgeoned to death on that dusty road.

Audrey Marie Nesbit, sitting naked in the dark remembered running to the bandstand, to the very center and screaming until she had no breath left – none for Angela and none for her mother.

Tree tops became a solace and Audrey spent more time in the forest. She also dove deep into the river of fantasy – a fantasy of Johnny Watson. She would imagine scenarios with Johnny and decorate them with detail so real it was difficult to know where reality faded into Audrey's misty mind. She needed to be loved just as Angela and Brenda – just as anyone does. Audrey left for school earlier than she needed so she could follow Johnny from a distance, and watch him walk with his friends Ralphie Pister and Buster Mose. She attended each home basketball game and sat near the entrance to the locker room to feel and smell him after a game. By the age of seventeen, Audrey had created such an elaborate story of their relationship that she ached as if her bones hurt from within.

So adept had Audrey become at remaining invisible and standing close to Johnny that she deluded herself into believing she really was invisible rather than simply unnoticed. Hungry, adept, and deluded Audrey, passing to class, reached her hand and took Johnny Watson's arm. No one was more surprised than she.

"Hey girl, whatcha doing?" Johnny said with that small mouthed smile full of puckishness and danger.

Audrey quickly replied, "Sorry, thought you were someone else" and escaped to her next class.

She was able to avoid Johnny for the rest of the day. She even took a short way home after school through a small patch of woods. Deep in thought and fantasy she did not see Johnny Watson leap from the underbrush. She halted. Quickly he grabbed the front of her blouse catching her bra as he did and forced her to the ground. He was on top of her but when he spread his legs, Audrey brought her knee up. Johnny Watson rolled off in pain and Audrey sprinted for home.

Audrey Marie Cook changed that moment in the woods. Gone were the fantasies, gone too was a certain innocence. School was a bit difficult those last two weeks of her senior year. Johnny would spend a second year as a senior. Audrey prepared for college and left in the fall. She did well at the University of Maine and majored in English. With her new degree she returned to Penobscot Mills and lived with her father and worked at the only bookstore.

Audrey still wanted love but she was resigned now and spent days deeper in the forest swinging on tree tops always longing and always alert until one day she saw a face in the neighboring tree. Rutherford Nesbit smiled a gentle and loving smile and asked politely if he could join her on her tree. She agreed and so began a real romance. They climbed trees together, took walks together, held hands and shared hopes and dreams. Rutherford was much better to Audrey than her imagination had ever been. Reality tasted good. One night Rutherford invited Audrey to dinner at his house. He made pot roast and they talked through the evening. He walked her home to her father's house but standing on the front steps Audrey could tell that Rutherford didn't know how to proceed. Audrey reached her hand to the nape of his neck and leaned up and kissed him. It wasn't as long a kiss as the one Brenda had given Johnny that day but it was sweet and the taste lingered. They were married soon after and Audrey Marie Nesbit moved into her husband's house.

The years till now had been blissful reality. Thirty-nine year old Audrey, sitting naked on the ninth level of their café, sighed and smiled at the wondrous taste of reality. She laughed at herself for all of the nights and days she had spent in fantasy. The front door jiggled and Audrey was wrenched from her thoughts. Had she forgotten to lock the door? Peering through the murk she could make out her pink panties hanging from the fichus tree by the front door. The hand that reached for them was familiar and Audrey breathed deeply. Creaking up the landings, Rutherford held her clothes. They hugged but Audrey clenched tighter than usual. Audrey Marie leaned back and a soggy drop of sheer joy splashed on naked toes.

# BUSTER MOZE

When you see a tree blanch, you know a storm is coming. It turns its leaves to the breeze, exposing the light green under side to the sky. It says, come, I am ready; give me what you will for I will stand with your breath in my face till I break.

The muted horn of soft jazz that inhabited the dim ninth level of the Tree Top Café would soon be shattered. That idyllic peace known to Audrey and Rutherford, a peace that supported them and helped them grow over the years, would be interrupted.

"The spiral staircase I found in Bangor won't work," said Rutherford.

"It's too expensive and besides...," Rutherford paused before continuing as if he was gathering the courage to jump into what may lurk in the deep end of the pool.

"Besides we lost our carpenter. Tony Martino was found floating in the river this morning – head bashed in, presumably by the pulp logs."

Audrey stared down to the first level and let a drop, distilled with the chemistry of sadness and horror, descend slowly until the splash could not be heard.

Tommy Ballenger approached Bank Northeast. The sight of Tony's body on the grassy bank bothered him. Watson had approached him after last night's party and demanded that he transfer Martino's home loan to his account. Tommy replied, "Yes, Mr. Watson." So to put Tony's death behind him, he would make the transfer of the Martino's home loan to Johnny Watson as directed. Sunday afternoon was no time to be doing this but Johnny was insistent and Tommy was not about to cross him. The door gave way and startled him. The bank's doors were always locked. He entered cautiously. Sun from the skylight created a glow akin to a solemn altar – an altar upon which the town's people could worship the money which Tommy helped to control.

"Ballenger, what are you doing?" barked Bernie Pittman. He and his brother Joe, superintendent of the mill, were smoking cigars and drinking Canadian Club.

"After the dinner last night, Johnny caught me and told me to transfer the Martino's home loan to him. I knew he had the money, so I'm here," replied a cautious Thomas J. Ballenger, Esq.

"What would he want with Martino's loan?" questioned Joe Pittman.

A look from Bernie silenced him. Both men began to stare at their glasses of whisky. They knew Tony Martino had been found that morning and suspicion would normally go to Watson. Pister would stonewall as usual and it would all blow over in time. A loan transfer could implicate the bank and Tony's widow would certainly find out. Johnny had done a great job for them over the years and as long as he didn't get too outrageous they left him alone. This could change the business and financial control they enjoyed over much of Penobscot Mills.

"Shall I make the transfer, Mr. Pittman?" asked Thomas J. Ballenger, Esq.

Bernie looked at Joe and drew his glass slowly to his lips.

"Naw, I'll take care of it"

"Ok, Mr. Pittman see you tomorrow," and Tommy slowly sidled for the door.

"Ballenger," Bernie barked. "You can call me Bernie from now on."

Tommy smiled. He was becoming closer to the center of power and he liked it.

"You bet, Bernie. See you Monday."

Joe turned to Bernie after Tommy had left.

"You think Watson did it? He's been a bully all his life and I'm sure a few pets have been sacrificed over the years, but murder? We can't afford to take that chance so we should begin to gradually wean Watson from the payroll."

"Gradual? I think we need to cut him off clean. He'll be mad, maybe even violent but we have to do it and I'm not transferring the loan," said Bernie.

Joe Pittman added, "Have you ever seen him really mad? He is pretty much out of control and I swear his eyes change color from blue to violet. The only other person who might be a problem would be…Rutherford."

Bernie barked again, "Can't be helped. Besides he's happy with his wife at that café making pancakes. He hasn't said anything for years. Maybe your suspicious are wrong. More whisky?"

As a former paymaster of the mill, Rutherford Nesbit knew a great deal about the deals Joe and Bernie made but it didn't concern him directly. He was free to get a loan for the café and to hire Tony Martino as often as he needed.

Tommy slipped out of the bank but not before he overheard everything. Thomas J. Ballenger, Esq. grinned and thought, *"I can use this information to gain more leverage."*

He walked into his house to find his wife Stephanie gone. He glanced in the backyard and up the street a bit. Then he dialed the phone.

"Can I come over? Stephanie is out."

Susan Beaumont opened the door and greeted Tommy with a kiss. He had renewed his relationship about a year or so after Stephanie and he moved back to Penobscot Mills. The carving on the cabin wall that Stephanie had found, *"Susan loves every BODY"* titillated him until he had to find her. Susan became his secretary at Bank Northeast much to the sadness of his wife.

After seeing Tony Martino's body on the river bank, Bobby Rosebush, David White, and Stephanie Ballenger agreed to meet at the cabin that afternoon. The breeze through pines and maples gently waved to the sky and sung a slow rhythmic dirge.

Stephanie was first to speak.

"Did you see the faces of the people around Tony this morning? They seemed sad but somehow resigned. It's not that they were callous, rather that they were numb."

"Only one side of his head was hit and I doubt it was the logs. Dave, did you and Tony have too much to drink last night?"

"No, he walked me home after dinner and said he wanted to think." David White wondered if he should have driven him home.

The sergeant leaned against the cabin wall and crossed his arms. "Tony and I were friends, hell we were all friends – even Dave until he went to Brunswick. I don't think Tony fell in the river. There appeared to be five blows to the left side of his head. Remember what Paul said about him seeing Watson kills pets – one, two, three, four, five. I can't prove it and Ralphie will be no help. I'm gonna look into this. I'm not sure how to begin though…" Bobby started to say.

"First place to start is Audrey at the Tree Top Café. We have become good friends and everybody goes there. She hears things and it's easy to eavesdrop in there," Stephanie offered. "Maybe we can get a tip."

David stared into the darkened cabin letting his imagination bring the ghost, Maude to him. She was scolding him for not doing more – for not standing up. It was Maude who warned him the night before – warned him something bad was about to happen. She didn't say to whom it would happen but with the morning David knew. He would help Bobby Rosebush. He'd call Ronnie Polk at the *Seven Seas Restaurant* and say he was staying a little longer.

Police Chief Ralph Pister was known as Ralphie to everyone. He inherited the job from Harold his father. Ralphie was the deputy at the time his father died of a heart attack. His long-time friendship with Johnny Watson was instrumental in getting the job. Johnny Watson was already working for the Pittman's, under the table so to speak and Bernie needed someone as chief to do as little as possible. That was perfect for Ralphie. He lived with his mother and oddly enough, Johnny.

Johnny's father took early retirement and went to live with his girlfriend in a town twenty five miles away. Johnny's mother lived alone. He had nothing good to say about her so when Ralphie's father died he moved in with the Pisters.

Ralphie sat on the front stoop drinking a beer Sunday afternoon. His cigarette drooped from his lips and its smoke snaked lazily up into his eyes which made him squint – but being Ralphie he was lazy enough to not mind so much.

"Johnny, you didn't kill Martino, did you?" Ralphie asked. It was a dangerous question and Ralphie was not steaming with courage. He looked at Johnny Watson watching for the viper to strike. He'd seen that many times over the years.

Johnny canted his head to the side until only one eye was staring at Pister. "Oh, hell no, Ralphie. I was with you, remember?" His smile was neither convincing nor telling.

"Actually Johnny you were gone for about an hour that night."

"I caught Ballenger and told him to transfer Martino's home loan to me…and I came back with a six pack of Bud." After a pause Johnny chuckled, "Maybe Buster Moze is back in town."

Ralphie's heart sank into a murky pond, fetid with trepidation. He choked on the stench of that remark.

The Tree Top Café was a hive Monday until close. Blueberry pancakes, bacon, eggs, potatoes, plenty of coffee and a maple-caramel muffin which Rutherford had created provided sufficient fuel for gossip. Stephanie was wrong. The town was not resigned to their fate. Tony Martino had been a main stay to hard working people. Audrey could hear slips of conversation which suggested Tony had been murdered and Johnny Watson's name was repeated often. The tough, the bully, who forced people to use Pittman Contracting and Lumber, swaggered in a persona and reputation that none dare cross.

Stephanie, Bobby, and David sat on the ninth level of the café and listened. The overlapping cacophony of sounds was like a circus calliope – too loud and out of tune to render a faithful performance, demanding "Come one, come all"-- until one spoken name stopped all mouths, "Buster Moze."

Years ago the town had blamed deaths, fires, and catastrophe on Buster Moze. An apparent inhabitant of Penobscot Mills whom no one could remember, remained an unseen boogie man. In a darkened nook, Johnny Watson listened. Buster Moze was back.

The hive of gossipers continued until closing. Audrey and Rutherford cleaned, cleared and prepared for tomorrow. Rutherford stepped down to the barber shop for a haircut. Audrey reached for the door and closed it in the same gentle manner she handled everything and everybody and slipped the key in the slot. Startled, she turned and Johnny Watson stood behind her with the same puckish smile of long ago.

"You know, Audrey, I wanted to tell you, I didn't kill Tony. No matter what you've heard here today. I've done some bad things but not this. I don't know why it means so much that you think better of me, but it does."

Johnny Watson walked up Main Street toward Bartlett's Drug Store where he intended to buy a pack of Lucky Strikes. No sooner did he enter, than the entire store went still. It was as if every hair on every arm dared not move; every eye stared blankly at nothing; every breath was held safe. He didn't care. He enjoyed the power that fear can provide and it provided well. He bought the cigarettes and left with the same smile which projected mirth and danger simultaneously. North on Beech Street he headed for the woods. He wore jeans, tennis shoes and a black t-shirt. He didn't seem to have grown past his teens. His father left when he was fifteen leaving him with a weak mother who never stood up for herself or for him. He was not sad to see his father go – he had been a difficult and cruel man, but he couldn't live with his mother.

Johnny entered the woods North of the High School and swam through the breeze that wafted between straight pines – bringing a scent that filled his lungs and allowed him to breathe easier. He enjoyed and employed the power of fear, but he was also lonely. People really thought he killed all those pets. He shook his head sadly. He had simply taken them deep into the forest, never to return.

Johnny Watson smiled again at the name Buster Moze. Most towns have a mysterious villain with whom the parents can threaten the children. Rarely taken seriously, the boogie man serves a purpose. Where the name Buster Moze came from and why it evoked so much genuine concern was unknown. People claim to have actually seen him and attributed all manner of heinous acts to him. Talks of howling in the forest at night and shadows strutting down vacant streets produced a reputation for the feared Buster Moze.

Johnny was immediately considered as Tony's murderer because he was almost always belligerent in nature and quick to anger and fight. When one spoken whisper of Buster Moze wafted upward in the *Tree Top Café*, a new possibility emerged and Johnny smiled slightly at the strange fate to have a fictitious figure claim the crime. Then Johnny wondered who really did kill Tony Martino?

Stephanie waited at the park for Audrey to ascend Beech Street on her walk home from the Café. Soon two bare foot women were dangling bare legs over the edge of the bandstand at the center of the park. Audrey was forced to recall a time when she and Angela McLean did the same thing. Stephanie and Audrey had become close friends soon after Tommy and Stephanie were married and moved to Penobscot Mills.

"We don't think Tony fell in the river. We think he was killed and dumped," said Stephanie. "We are going to the mortuary this afternoon to look at his body."

Audrey looked at Stephanie with a look of disbelief and surprise.

"You wanna come?"

Audrey did not answer.

"Do you believe Tony died of an accident?"

Finally Audrey replied, "No I don't but I'm not sure it was Johnny. I've known him for many years and yes he's been in trouble and maybe stolen some pets but he just told me he didn't kill Tony."

Stephanie watched four legs swing aimlessly over the white bandstand as carefree and effortless as the summer day they were enjoying – no cares, no anxiety. "Who was Buster Moze?"

Slowly, Audrey replied. "Years ago there was apparently someone named Buster Moze. People claim to have seen him. I think I saw him and Johnny and Ralphie walking together but no record has been found. I don't know but there were suspicious fires, dead animals, and vandalism years ago all attributed to Buster Moze. Then Angela was killed and Old Blisters was killed and Johnny's father left to live with his girlfriend. Most of it stopped. I don't know." Audrey hung her head then peered up at Stephanie who said, "I didn't' know Tony well. What was he like?"

"Tony was a good carpenter and started his business with the help of old Bill Mackenzie. His biggest competitor was Pittman Lumber and Construction. The lumber was more expensive for Tony so he had to charge his customers more. The Pittman brothers controlled most of the finances in Penobscot

Mills. We gave him the job of renovating the warehouse and constructing the Tree Top Café. For some reason, we had no trouble with the Pittman brothers and gave Tony as much business as we could. In the end Tony was forced to go to work for the mill making half of what he had in his own business. "

Stephanie began to relate the story of Paul McLean's letter to David White and the discussion the night before at the cabin.

"Paul McLean thinks Johnny killed his sister, Angela," whispered Stephanie. "Did you know her?"

"We were two years apart but we were friends. We would sit right here just like we are now. She was intellectually limited but she was sweet and innocent. She was also a great dancer." The words wafted up to rest in the shelter and safety of the parabola roof of the old bandstand – keeping Angela company in the memory of those little girl squeals so long ago.

Audrey declined the offer to visit the mortuary and in the end only Bobby Rosebush and Stephanie Ballenger dared approach. As Bobby led Stephanie down a flight of stairs to the embalming room their hands touched for a moment – knuckle to knuckle, radius to radius, ulna to ulna, their forearms trading hairs and they turned face to face. Both turned away quickly and proceeded down. Formaldehyde entered Stephanie's nostrils and caused her to choke. The mortician's son had served with the sergeant in Nam, so access was granted. Observing the body it could be seen that only the left side of his face was bruised and the bruises were most evident. Bobby counted at least four perhaps five distinct circular blows. "Just like what Paul said about seeing Johnny Watson kill an animal," whispered Bobby. The funeral would be Wednesday morning. Audrey and Rutherford would attend and the Tree Top Café would be closed. Tony Martino's coffin would also be closed.

A small town is no place for sleuthing, although secrets and hidden trysts were kept, but asking questions, visiting the mortuary, and especially talking to one's husband can keep everyone well informed. Indeed, Tommy Ballenger knew practically everything the group was doing. He kept an attentive gaze as Stephanie reviewed what they knew.

The evening after Tony's funeral Tommy was talking quite a bit. He bragged about calling the bank president, by name and how close he was getting to the real power in Penobscot Mills. He turned to Stephanie and blurted, "Do you know what I heard? Joe said that when Johnny gets really mad his eyes change color from blue to violet; not that I ever want to see him mad."

During a lull Stephanie slowly asked, "Who was Buster Moze?"

Tommy looked at his wife and sighed. Finally Tommy said, "I'm not sure but I know we saw him when we were young. He was always with Johnny Watson and sometimes Ralphie was with them. We never wanted to get close to them but many people also say they saw him too but didn't really know him. After unexplained fires and vandalism he got a reputation and even the missing pets were often attributed to him."

Tommy stopped suddenly and stared at the blank television screen as if studying his reflection. After a while he got up and switched it on.

Thursday morning, the day after the funeral, Bobby and Stephanie decided to take a walk through the woods North of town. Stephanie was almost certain that Tommy was seeing Susan Beaumont but ignoring the issue was easier than confrontation. Tommy was at work and Bobby was at hand. She was surprised at how comfortable she felt with him – the hardnosed Marine, tough talking, direct, and yet he was always respectful as if his mother's teaching was ever in his mind.

Tromping one foot then the other, scraping on undergrowth, secure in the knowledge that poison ivy had not reached northern Maine, Bobby and Stephanie hiked. The Marine and Physical Education Teacher made a good pair. With Stephanie in the lead, Bobby noticed the glistening of sweat on Stephanie's thighs and T-shirt; with Bobby in the lead, Stephanie enjoyed the scent of an active man. The sweat, the woods and a pair of heart beats became a chemical laboratory to distil hope. The brief grazing of arms and knuckles in the mortuary invited a possibility. The partnership they felt suggested an opportunity. Soon they were side to side, arm to arm and coming up a rise. They gave in to the natural instinct to grasp each other's hand as they descended the small hill to a depression in the forest floor.

They had driven so deep into the forest, they knew little about their location. Bobby and Stephanie stood face to face. Stephanie took one small graceful step forward and heard a crack – not the crunch of leaves but a decided snap. The couple looked around them and began to realize they were in the midst of a ghoulish graveyard of dead animals. There could have easily been a hundred skeletons in this clearing. Horror was the emotion shared by both.

Bobby and Stephanie returned to town in silence. Sergeant, Robert Oliver Rosebush had seen carnage in Viet Nam but this was work produced by senseless rage. Was this Johnny or Buster? He needed to talk to Ralphie and it might not be easy.

The tile floor shone clean, bright and medicinal; wax invaded the nostrils and choked the lungs. No one was available at the Penobscot Mills Police Station. Through a crack in a door, Bobby saw Ralphie dozing in his chair.

"Ralphie!" barked Bobby.

Chief Ralphie Pister slowly opened his eyes. "What do you want, Rosebush?"

The presence of the Marine was formidable and Ralphie sat up and rested his arms on the desk.

"Just want of ask a couple of questions, Ralphie. Did Johnny Watson really play cards with you all night?"

Ordinarily Ralphie would stonewall in the same disinterested sleepy ploy he had used so often. This time Ralphie considered the question. He had his own doubts. Actually asking Johnny if he had killed Martino was risky but he needed to ask because he knew more about Johnny than anyone.

"He went out for about an hour but he caught Ballenger after the Pittman's dinner party and told him to transfer Martino's home loan to him."

"He could have had enough time to kill Tony don't you think?" The Sergeant tilted his head just slightly and waited for a response."

"Maybe but he came back with a six-pack of Bud."

The Marine Sergeant maintained a steady glare then asked, "When was the last time you saw Buster Moze?"

Ralphie went white, his mouth drying, his tongue sticking to the roof of his mouth. Quietly and slowly he responded. "I haven't seen him in years – not since we graduated from high school."

"Could he be back?" asked the Sergeant.

"I hope not but I asked Johnny who could have killed Martino and he said, 'maybe Buster Moze is back.' I hope…" Ralphie's words trailed off and his eyes turned to the wall.

Paul McLean, Bobby Rosebush, David White, Stephanie Ballenger, and Audrey Nesbit sat on the very edge of the bandstand a summer afternoon in July. "What do we know?" asked the Sergeant.

"Tony left me at 9:30 Saturday night and walked home which should have taken him five or six minutes to reach his house," began David. "We had not had too much to drink, perhaps some red wine to go with the lasagna but not so much to make him trip."

"Johnny approached me and said he didn't kill Tony and I believe him. I've known him the longest and yes he's probably done some bad things but why would he even approach me if he had done it?" offered Audrey.

Stephanie added, "Johnny told Tommy to transfer the Martino home loan to him to protect Tony from foreclosure by Bank Northeast."

"Stephanie and I saw five round marks on Tony, all on the left side of his head, right Steph?"

"Yes that's right. We also found about a hundred skeletons of small animals in the woods."

The Sergeant began, "Ralphie said that Johnny was out for about an hour that night which could have given him just enough time to kill Tony and dump his body but not much more than that. When I mentioned Buster Moze he went white. I think Ralphie believes Buster is back and so does Johnny."

"But Johnny tried to rape me my senior year in high school," Audrey interjected.

Everyone turned to her with surprise and compassion in their eyes. After an uncomfortable pause, Stephanie asked, "Audrey, what color were his eyes when he was on top of you?"

"Blue-red, violet; I can still see them staring at me sometimes."

"There seems to be a confusing factor in all of this," Stephanie continued. "Maybe Buster Moze has been behind this all along. People swear they have seen him in the past and the violet eye color might be associated with him, not Johnny. I think Buster tried to rape you, not Johnny. That would explain his comment to you the other day."

"Could be Buster Moze is back. No murders since Angela McLean and Old Blisters, then Tony is killed. Paul, are you sure you saw Johnny Watson or could it have been Buster Moze who killed Angela?" Bobby Rosebush asked.

After a pause Paul replied, "Yeah it could have been."

Under the bandstand, deep in the dirt with greasy fingers and filthy trousers, Buster Moze listened and seethed.

"Today is Friday so why don't we take a break tomorrow and meet at the cabin around six. It will still be light enough. I'll bring a bottle," Bobby Rosebush suggested. They all agreed.

Johnny Watson grasped the brass handle to Bernie Pittman's office at the bank on Saturday morning and twisted. His routine was to collect his pay in cash each week from Bernie. Cigar smoke was evident and Joe and Bernie were there.

"Well hello, gentlemen. Do I get double pay this week?" asked Johnny.

Bernie spoke. "Watson, we're done. Here's your six hundred but that's it. You're not needed anymore."

Johnny Watson's jaw clenched and his eyes squinted until almost no pupil could be seen. Bernie Pittman's door contained a full panel of frosted glass. Launching himself, Johnny smashed through the glass and landed on the floor. Pulling himself up he turned and spoke the same words he had spoken to the Lizard on Halloween those many years ago, "You don't want to do this," and he left.

He motioned to Tommy to meet him outside. During the commotion of the broken glass, Tommy slipped out of the bank.

"Ballenger, I just got fired and you're probably next. What's going on?"

For Tommy, loyalty was situational and was influenced by the person with whom he was talking. While Bernie was his boss, Johnny was dangerous. He told Watson everything his wife had said the past week.

Johnny Watson's walk became stiff and stilted the further away from the bank he traveled. He whispered to himself, through his fingers that waved in front of his mouth.

*Can't let this happen and won't. After all I've done to this town...won't let them get away with it. Rosebush and that girl, gonna get them both and that pansy White. Five slams to his head. To your head DADDY. Dear, dear Daddy...*

His demeanor suddenly shifted.

*"Daddy don't...don't! Please, oh it's gonna hurt. No, please no. I'll be good...* then shifted again *...damn bastard always trying to screw me up. Glad you're gone...glad glad. We need to kill something. What, who why why. No Buster. Please no.*

*Shut up! This needs to be really big – really big and horrible. Come on Johnny think, you're gonna help us. We are gonna do this together this time. Open your eyes.*

The troop wended their way through the forest and approached the cabin. This place had become almost sacred to Stephanie. It was where she was first introduced to Penobscot Mills, where she learned of Johnny Watson's sins, and of Buster Moze the villain. First Stephanie then Audrey, soon David and Bobby and finally Paul who remained reticent, stepped upon the porch. The waning light composed a pavane for Tony and the town of Penobscot Mills. The clouds were heavy and close and rain threatened but the group swigged the liquor and laughed. None of them noticed two rusty brackets newly installed on either side of the empty door frame. Then the rain came and even though the porch roof was largely intact the group went inside.

David White was having trouble concentrating because the ghost, Maude, kept entering the cabin, vomiting soil, and pointing toward the back wall. David should have seen this as a warning but whisky had taken charge of him.

"Dave," slurred the Sergeant. "What's up?"

David White could no longer keep it in. He broke down in sobs and in a jerky fashion told his story. "Since my Aunt Dot left I've been alone and I am used to it. But there are ghosts in that house – ghosts of hers and of mine who talk to me and befriend me. It's how I write. They tell me their stories and I take dictation. It's a bit disgusting. First they vomit dirt, the dirt from their graves—black and full of mold, and then they tell me their story. Maude, one of Aunt Dot's ghosts is here now and she keeps point to the rear wall."

No one knew what to say. Stephanie had a look of pity.

It seemed to Stephanie that Brunswick had been ages ago and the dim glimmer of recollection barely shown though the murk that inhabited the cabin. She remembered fondly his Aunt Dot, and Evan – the shy clumsy false starts at conversation in high school halls and the hint of trapped desperation behind David's eyes. Pity was not a just emotion to feel for David. He took what had been bequeathed to him and survived. No, pity was the right emotion to feel for her. *"Trapped, she thought? Yes I know trapped."* Then she glanced at the arms of the Sergeant and his happy sure way of engaging life. He was honest and uncomplicated – so unlike her Tommy. *"There's got to be a second chance."*

Audrey was feeling a slight loss. Rutherford had not gone along with the sleuthing and clandestine conversations among the group. It created a break between them. This had not happened before and it bothered her. The fact that the investigation had floated memories of infatuation with Johnny Watson and the possible/probable implication in murder, twisted her thoughts and made her ache for Rutherford even more. There was no muted horn of soft jazz in this cabin. She needed to get back to him.

Paul sat cross legged in the very center of the cabin and looked through the open door. All those years he suffered, all those years he grieved for his sister, all those years he blamed himself for not saying anything in support of Angela. What could a ten year old brother do? Tears came in the same small drizzle of rain on the porch and he sighed for the love of Angela, his sweet artistic sister. The thought of confronting Watson drew him to near panic.

The cabin, which had turned to the gloom of early evening, became quickly darker. A make-shift door had been slammed against the frame and a two by four slid into the brackets. Two wide mouthed mason jars full of gasoline were emptied and a match was tossed. Flames quickly erupted up the wall of this ancient tinder box, trapping the group inside. The liquor impeded the reaction of even the Marine.

The porch was quickly ablaze and the flames reached into the cabin through the empty windows – reaching with feathered arms to catch and arm or leg and drag it onto the porch. That cabin, that old forgotten and abused woman screamed an obscenity and soon became eyes and mouth of regret, and whisky, and sex and years of longing.

There seemed to be no escape. David pointed to the rear wall and said that this was the weakest spot, "trust me." Bobby looked at David and David nodded. Bobby and David launched their shoulders into the wall and crashed through. The sudden rush of air drew the flames quickly into the cabin. Paul escorted Stephanie and Audrey through the exit.

A shot from a snub-nosed .38 ripped through Bobby's left bicep. There stood a soiled creature – greasy fingers, contorted face and a guttural voice which said, "kneel down." Buster Moze was enraged, fueled by the years of cruelty. His violet eyes became brighter than the raining night. He held the gun in his left hand and a hatchet in his right. He threw the hatchet which caught David in his thigh. Then with a grin through a dripping mouth pointed the gun at Audrey who had backed against the wall with no escape.

A thrash of leaves and branches and a definite thud startled the creature and announced the arrival of Rutherford Nesbit. He had traveled through the tree tops in a desperate attempt to save is beloved Audrey.

The creature was surprised for only moment at the sight of a man plummeting to earth. Rutherford found that he was not quite up to the task at hand so he tossed something to Bobby Rosebush. The Marine flipped the silver object until he held it between his thumb and finger then threw it with the skill of a trained soldier. The object pierced the creature's left eye. He shuddered, shot wildly and fell to his knees then off to his side. David White recognized his sharpened butter knife which he stole from Tim Nightingale's roadhouse. It was the knife that Tommy Ballenger used to stab Rutherford many years before – the knife Rutherford had kept in a wooden box on top of his walnut wardrobe.

The creature was still. The rain drizzled down his face and into is opened right eye. Then as if washing away the madness his right eye faded to pure blue and his face was that of Johnny Watson. He smiled a small smile and said, "Buster what have you done to us?" and died.

The group returned to town. Due to the clearing around the cabin and drenching rain, the fire would not threaten the forest but the flames licked the old girl who had endured so many emotions and assaults. She could only sigh and smile and return to the forest from which she had come.

Paul said to Rutherford, "It was fortunate you came along when you did."

"I didn't just come along. I knew what was happening. I knew Johnny was fired by the Pittman brothers and would be enraged. Besides protecting Audrey, I had my own score to settle with the Watson/Moze creature. My older brother,

Millard Nesbit, was a disappointment to my folks. He lived for years at the town dump and was killed with Angela McLean."

"You mean Old Blisters was your brother?" gasped Stephanie.

"Yes, and he liked to climb trees just as Audrey and I do. I guess it's a family trait," replied Rutherford Nesbit wrapping his arms around Audrey.

Audrey, Rutherford, Bobby, Paul, Stephanie, and David visited Ralphie Pister in the hospital. He had been shot with his own snub-nosed .38 in the hip. Raphie began to tell a story only he and Johnny Watson's mother knew.

"Johnny's back, belly and genitals are littered with maybe a hundred razor slices and cigarette burns. His father was very thorough. At some point Johnny split into Buster and Johnny. It was Buster Moze who killed Angela, "Old Blisters," and Tony."

"But we've all seen Buster and you and Johnny walking together," Paul said.

"I know but he was only Johnny to me. He was good to my mom and me and only when he was really angry did he seem to be different."

The Tree Top Café was closed and seated in the darkened ninth level were: Paul, Audrey, Rutherford, David, Stephanie and Bobby. "How could we have seen Buster when he never really existed?" asked the logical and clear-headed Marine.

David White sat cross-legged in a darker corner of the ninth level and spoke softly.

"I think I know. I like sitting in the dark alone, because I'm never alone. There are too many voices in my head. My Aunt's ghosts, my ghosts and thoughts swirl around in the dark. At first they were just shadows I thought I saw out of the corner of my eye. Night after night alone in the dark the feeling of abandonment slowly replaced my blood with its own formaldehyde. Living alone for so long I've become comfortable with those thoughts. We all talk to ourselves. I saw my Aunt Dot tap those black and white photos and smile and whisper and converse with those long dead. After she left me, I began doing the same thing. I know the ghosts are not real but in a sense they are. How else could I know just where the weakest spot was on that cabin wall? Maude told me.

"In a town where people believe in superstition, they want to explain why bad things happen. And Penobscot Mills may feel a twinge of guilt for not investigating Angela and Old Blister's murder."

David looked at Paul whose eyes were filling. Paul remembered the guilt that forced him to write the letter to David.

"So," David continued, "fear and guilt in a dark alley will conjure almost anything, even Buster Moze."

Audrey Marie sat with her bare legs thrust through the bars of the railing, dangling nine levels from the ground. "Yes," she spoke. "I lived my life so steeped in fantasy that anything was real for me and when Angela died I just jumped into my own river and floated away."

"But why now, why did Buster re-appear now?" asked Stephanie who was finding it difficult to grasp all that was being said – as difficult as it was for Bobby Rosebush, the clear thinking Marine Sergeant.

Paul drew a breath, exhaled through a besotted throat and rumbled, "Because you came back, David. We began to talk and we began to believe and make noise in this town and Buster heard us."

Paul's thoughts were of Angela, his sister – without guile, artistic, free and innocent. All this time he grieved and felt guilty when he was truly blameless. He looked a Audrey, Angela's friend and she nodded as if to give her blessing as well.

Ralphie Pister was be pensioned off by the Pittman brothers and could continue his lazy happy life. Rutherford and Audrey went back to work at the Tree Top Café. Tony Martino's wife became the manager of the café allowing Rutherford and Audrey more time to ride their trees. Tommy Ballenger and Stephanie divorced and Tommy married Susan Beaumont. Paul decreased his drinking and became a full time janitor of the elementary school. He was beloved by the students who descended the stairs to the boiler room to show him their art work and listen to the stories he read. David White returned to Brunswick in seclusion with his ghosts, to live a life with which he had become most comfortable.

Retired Marine Gunnery Sergeant, Robert Oliver Rosebush married Stephanie and became the police chief of that little town in northern Maine.

A couple of last questions were posed on the ninth level of the café that day after Johnny Watson died. David asked, "I wonder if Mr. Watson knows Johnny is dead? Or if anyone knows where his is? By the way, we all called him Mr. Watson. I don't even know his first name."

Rutherford responded, "As paymaster for the mill I knew his first name was John." Then he choked and said. "But I know the men all called him Buster."